WRITTEN IN LIGHT

AND OTHER FUTURISTIC TALES

JEFF YOUNG

eSpec Books
Pennsville, NJ

PUBLISHED BY
eSpec Books LLC
Danielle McPhail, Publisher
PO Box 242,
Pennsville, New Jersey 08070
www.especbooks.com

ISBN: 978-1-949691-37-5
ISBN (eBook): 978-1-949691-36-8

"Written in Light." *Writers of the Future 26*, edited by K. D. Wentworth, Galaxy Press, LLC, 2010, pp. 385-420.
"The Janus Choice." *If We Had Known*, edited by Mike McPhail, eSpec Books, LLC, 2017, pp. 51-68.
"No Visitors Beyond This Point." *Trail of Indiscretion: Special Edition Two*, edited by Brian Koscienski, Fortress Publishing, Inc, 2016, pp. 3-12.
"A Talent Beyond My Talents." *Fantastic Futures 13*, edited by Robert Waters and James R. Stratton, Padwolf Publishing, 2013, pp. 159-171.
"Blankets." *By Other Means*, edited by Mike McPhail, Dark Quest Books, LLC, 2011, pp. 25-34.
"The Luminous Blind Spot." *Trail of Indiscretion*, 2006, pp. 15–19.
"Reading Between the Lines." *In a Flash 2016*, edited by Danielle Ackley-McPhail, eSpec Books, LLC, 2016, pp. 36-38.
"Liar's Globe." *The Realm Beyond #4*, 2012, pp. 51-55.

Copyediting: Greg Schauer and John L. French
Interior Design: Danielle McPhail
Cover Design and Art Modification: Mike McPhail, McP Digital Graphics
Cover Art: Tithi Luadthong, ID - 1207264096, www.shutterstock.com
Accent Credit: floral_lines © sanyal, www.fotolia.com

In Appreciation

THANK YOU TO ALL OF THE TEACHERS, FAMILY, FRIENDS, AND others who told me to keep writing—look, I did listen, kept at it, and here's the proof.

THANKS TO DYANE, THE BRIGHTEST SPOT IN THE DARK DAYS OF THE Pandemic, who had to listen to me ponder and grouse about the necessities of writing and rewriting these stories. Your support and presence made this year much more bearable.

THANKS, ONCE AGAIN, TO THE FOLKS AT ESPEC BOOKS WHO MADE this possible and came back to publish yet another book of mine. Your support helps me remain focused on creating more fiction. Missed you this year and looking forward to seeing more of you as soon as possible.

THANKS IN ADVANCE TO YOU, THE READER, FOR PURCHASING THIS book. I hope you enjoy the ride. I had fun writing down the words and worlds for you to experience.

JY

Contents

Written in Light

For a moment, Zoi'ahmets stood as still as the tree the wickurn resembled, watching as the unknown creature stumbled backward from her. Perhaps it was the fact that Zoi'ahmets rose twice its height, her triple conjoined trunks, or the orange eye that she swiveled in its direction. *Two podia, how could it manage like that?* So inefficient in dealing with gravity, unstable surfaces, and even the strain over time on such a small surface area, certainly nothing like Zoi'ahmets's designs. She had so little time to be certain that everything remained prepared for the Diversiform Dispute judging, and what in Winter happened here? The cognition engine finally linked with the translator nailed to her bark. Only then did she grasp that the sounds striking the translator were attempts at communication.

Amazingly, the intruder turned its back completely on Zoi'ahmets and began to dig through the grass—a very anti-survival trait in an unresolved situation. Perhaps it lost something. She fed its image into the cognition engine, which identified the creature as a *human*. Trying to imagine what it might be searching for, the wickurn cast about with all her eyes looking over the thick verdure of the pampas and nearby bushes. *There.* Something black and lumpy with a short set of straps hung in the top of a shrub nearby. One branch reached for it as another gently spun the human around and faced it toward its property. The human awkwardly trudged through the grass. Zoi'ahmets gently handed it the case. It spared a moment to eye its benefactor thoughtfully and then dropped gracelessly to the ground to open the case. The human quickly extracted a silver device which, when clipped behind its ear, opened up like a flower. The shiny metallic petals spun and clicked restlessly in the afternoon sunlight. Another device fit about its neck and a third nestled in the center of its hand. Then Zoi'ahmets finally heard the human begin to speak.

"______ wickurn ______ about 3 meters ______ seems to be looking out for me. ______ see why it's here. Since I'm as far into the Disputed zone as I am ______ ______ ______ ______. Can't understand why it hasn't ______ with me yet."

"Communicated?" Zoi'ahmets offered as she pulled herself slowly to the human.

"Yeah, actually," the being stammered.

"You were not exactly making intelligible sounds until just a moment ago."

"And you were pretending to be a tree! No, I'm sorry, you are a tree. You can't help that. I guess I just never expected you to move."

"Why would I require help if I am in my natural state?"

"Look, this isn't going well. You're one of the workers on this Diversiform Dispute, and I'm obviously keeping you from your job. I apologize for startling you, if that's what I did." It took a deep breath and continued, "I'm Kiona. I'm ... a student of the art of photography. I rode the ground vehicle over there until it stopped. Then the flight craft following us crashed into a tree. I'm so sorry to disturb you. I only wanted to learn more about the Disputed Zone."

It bowed slightly in Zoi'ahmets' direction, focusing two green eyes on her.

Zoi'ahmets raised a branch, and its eye could see there were fragments of debris at the base of a windrake tree. Flight craft? That could simply be a result of the inaccuracy of the translator. In fact, now that Zoi'ahmets looked at the wreckage, it bore a resemblance to an automated sampling drone. The small craft hung, entangled in the net of branches, its weight dragging down the tendrils and breaking them. Looking where indicated, she could see a surface sampling rover. A makeshift seat mounted to the top of the six-wheeled drone sat directly over the solar panel. Kiona must have ridden the sampler until it ran out of power. The aerial drone would have lost its guidance and then crashed. *Could it really be that stupid, or could this be deliberate?* Zoi'ahmets wondered.

She turned back to the human in front of her. Perhaps an introduction, "I am Zoi'ahmets Calinve, chief architect of the Wickurn

Diversiform entrant in this Dispute." Gently tipping forward, she returned the bow as much as she could manage. Kiona backed up another step.

"I am so sorry. I had no idea this is your environment. I never wanted to harm it."

Zoi'ahmets cocked a lower eye toward it. "But you had no problem entering the contested area to gain images of the Dispute — did you? You appear to have subverted a sampling drone to carry you. It's surprising the drone made it this far."

With that, she began the typical spiraling walk of a wickurn toward the drone. All the while, she thought to herself, *I must find a way to get this thing out of here as quickly as possible.* She'd heard that humans were allowed onto this Dispute World and didn't know how she felt about the imposition. Now she had one interrupting her work. For a second, she considered that her opponents might have put the intruder here to hinder her.

Kiona started after her, but the wickurn found herself waiting as the human pulled at one of the coverings on its feet and set to work on something lodged in an ankle. When it held the annoyance to the light to look at it, Zoi'ahmets dropped a branch eye to view it as well.

"Caltrop seed," she said. "Something I designed that will allow animals to transport seeds. Helps to propagate various bushes. Basically, harmless, but in your case perhaps annoying." *Also, a distraction,* thought Zoi'ahmets, *instead let's find out why you are here.* "Let us have a look at *your* conveyance."

Her eyes studied Kiona for a moment as her branch, vane leaves unfurling, drifted across Kiona's shoulder to urge it along. She pushed aside rising annoyance and moved forward.

While the human trotted beside Zoi'ahmets as the wickurn's three root clusters rolled through the thick grasses, Zoi'ahmets took a moment to access the cognition engine and review the biology reports for humanity. Just to be thorough, she'd made certain to download a full bio-summary of all the judges' species and anyone who might be visiting the Dispute. Thank Summer, there were no immediate concerns regarding her bio-system.

Looking briefly at Kiona, Zoi'ahmets suddenly realized this was a female of their species and estimated her age at about twelve winters. At first glance, Kiona appeared to be in good health. However inappropriate, one of the humans may have decided to take a firsthand look at the entrants to the Dispute rather than waiting as tradition dictated.

Zoi'ahmets looked briefly down at Kiona, considering her again. Humanity had joined the galactic community later than most, and there were concerns among the established species. Humans bred faster than most galactics and still had not modified themselves to limit their numbers. In a community where the primary means of gaining additional planetary growing room was based upon the ability to create effective complete environments for the Diversiform Disputes, most participants learned by modifying their homes and themselves first. Humanity had done a remarkable job of terra-forming numerous worlds, but the issue of their unregulated propagation still remained.

Because Zoi'ahmets's contemplation slowed her pace, Kiona darted ahead of the wickurn toward the crash of the airborne sampling drone. With a quick glance, Zoi'ahmets noted that it was made of tensioned monomolecular fabric. The remains of a nearby wing swinging overhead seemed to be mostly gas cells with monomole struts. Looking back toward the ground sampler, unease made her stomachs churn. Zoi'ahmets studied Kiona for a moment. Was the human not telling her everything? What was going on here? Did she have time for this?

Zoi'ahmets paused in consideration and looked up at the sky. Reflexively, she called up a weather survey. The cognition engine brought up a real-time satellite map displaying the relatively calm but cloudy current weather and a storm front moving toward their location. Perhaps Kiona hadn't intended to be out for long, or perhaps being trapped here was all part of the plan. The transmission faded out as Zoi'ahmets became lost in her own considerations.

In the meantime, the human walked about the surface drone. Kiona pulled out another strap-bearing bag from the grass and rummaged through it. Her hand showed through a hole in the bottom as her face skewed, and she murmured something that the translator box didn't quite register. She turned to Zoi'ahmets.

"Something ate my food, and the only thing left is a snack square. Hopefully, it wasn't anything of yours that might be poisoned by it."

That briefly perplexed Zoi'ahmets. It certainly wasn't the type of comment someone with a nefarious purpose would make unless Kiona's intent was to deliberately mislead her.

Zoi'ahmets watched as Kiona crawled further among the pampas, where she found a round container twice the size of her palm and pushed that into her black bag. "The rover is ruined," Kiona commented.

Sadly, the human appeared to be right. Slipping into a gully after it lost power and communication with the satellite grid, the drone snapped two of its three axels.

Zoi'ahmets noticed that the base of Kiona's leg where it emerged from the grass was no longer the same color as the rest of her. It was the same foot from which she'd withdrawn the caltrop seed.

Zoi'ahmets reached into a mouth. Probing gently past her gullet into one of the xylem spaces, she pulled out a round cylinder. She shook out the tiny arrow-shaped chenditi that clung to the sides. They landed on her lower trunk. Zoi'ahmets's large orange eye watched as the chenditi absorbed enough solar energy to fill the lift cells in their small bodies by splitting moisture from the air into hydrogen and oxygen. Separately, the little creatures were mere animals. A small swarm equipped with send/receive components acted as a collective intelligence.

Kiona stopped her scavenging to watch as the swarm lifted into the air. One half of each arrowhead was dark black, and the opposite canted at an angle covered with a shiny prismatic surface. Zoi'ahmets noticed that when Kiona stood up from the rover, she favored her left leg.

At first, Kiona shied as the chenditi flitted about her but was apparently familiar with their ability to do chemical and medical diagnostics. They quickly surrounded the human, and she held her arms out from her body as they spun about her. "Like a cloud of butterflies." Kiona laughed at the image. She drew her gaze back to Zoi'ahmets. Her glance was quick, and her lips slid to one side, a slight breeze lifting her shoulder-length blonde fur. "I do know what they're for. What do you think is wrong with me?"

"That is what they will tell us."

"Will you tell me, though?"

Zoi'ahmets was completely taken aback by that comment. Had they not established a basis for trust? Was this further evidence of malicious intent? Was the human aware that Zoi'ahmets harbored suspicions concerning her motives? Further queries of the cognition engine suddenly made her realize something she missed earlier—this was a sapling, not an adult. Zoi'ahmets was briefly off-balance trying to align her own species's view with that of human development. Wickurn budlings were given enough of the parent's memories to be instantly viable and then grew into mobility while developing a unique persona. They hardly compared to a species whose young were born with a tabula rasa. Human adults gave trust to younglings as they provided evidence that they were developed enough to earn it. Zoi'ahmets formed a suitable reply as the data from the chenditi medical assessment came through. "I have no reason not to be honest with you."

Kiona shook her head. "Typical adult. You didn't answer my question."

She reached into her pack and pulled out a white-wrapped square. Peeling back an edge, she began to eat. Zoi'ahmets devoted part of her attention to Kiona and the rest to the results. Most of Kiona's biochemistry was a mystery to Zoi'ahmets, but the chenditi found chemicals that were out of balance for the information the cognition engine carried about typical humans. Hormone levels were elevated, and there was an odd reaction with something called histamines as well. The girl's core temperature registered two degrees above standard, and there were abnormal red streaks and swelling in the area where Kiona removed the seed.

"You have an infection, possibly caused by your injury and possibly due to exposure to microorganisms in the air. Do you have an emergency kit? My medicines and those the chenditi can produce will not help your physiology," Zoi'ahmets stated.

The chenditi swarm came to rest, clinging to the bark of her trunk, their small bodies twitching and jerking as they arranged themselves to soak up the maximum light.

Kiona stopped eating the snack square, brow furrowing slightly. She reached into her bag and pulled out the round container she'd rescued from the wreckage. Prying back a corner, she poked and prodded at the interior. A few chenditi flew to look over her shoulder, and she held up the contents one by one to the small creatures.

"Those will not help. Can you walk?" Zoi'ahmets asked as the chenditi returned. Kiona pushed herself to her feet, leaning against the wickurn's rough bark.

Watching Kiona, Zoi'ahmets' mind raced. What should she do now? It would take valuable time to return the human to the Judging Area. Would Zoi'ahmets be given any dispensation toward additional time to test her results? She felt confident in the current development of the biosphere but was reluctant to give up any additional time. Then she considered the infection. Her opponents in the Diversity Dispute, the tio chaundon, used virii to control certain developmental aspects of their biosphere. Were they infecting Zoi'ahmets' biosphere? Could this be a deliberate attempt at sabotage?

She tried to use the satellite uplink but received only the hum of static. A frisson of panic ran up her trunks, making Zoi'ahmets dig her roots into the topsoil. Was she in danger from Kiona? Had the human cut Zoi'ahmets off from the satellite net, or had the tio chaundon?

Zoi'ahmets quelled the desire to distance herself from the human. All the same, she could not abandon another sentient in need. There was also the consideration that the judges would inevitably be made aware of what transpired here. Her choices narrowed considerably. At least by accompanying the human, she could observe Kiona and ensure the girl did no damage to the environment. Otherwise, if a tio chaundon virus infected the human, Zoi'ahmets couldn't afford to have Kiona perish under her protection.

"How far?" Kiona asked, looking toward the horizon.

Zoi'ahmets placed two branches on Kiona's shoulders, gently spinning the girl around ninety degrees to the right. "Thirty-five kilometers to the Judging Area."

"Oh," was her soft reply. "Can't we go to your base of operations?"

Again, Zoi'ahmets found herself wondering, did the human plan to sabotage the biosphere by destroying Zoi'ahmets's work base? She answered quickly, "There's nothing there to help you. Wickurn don't have the same physical requirements as humans. There must be an enclave set aside for your kind at the Judging Area."

Kiona turned away, looking back toward her original position. "Great. My parents are going to love this. Look, I swear, I never intended for this to happen, and I really hope that this will have no effect on the outcome of the Dispute. I really just wanted to get some images—well, I really wanted to see, and nobody was going to let me near anything."

Zoi'ahmets pondered that revelation for a few seconds before urging Kiona into motion toward the far-off enclave.

"Perhaps you do not understand how wickurn look upon the Disputes. I know that other races actively attempt to fine-tune their strategies as the Dispute occurs. Wickurn feel that if our design has enough viable integrity, it will succeed."

The grass rustled with their passing. Zoi'ahmets glanced briefly at the map that the cognition engine displayed in her mind's eye. There were two ridges to traverse. Although Zoi'ahmets's gait uphill would cost them time, it would be quicker than following the level ground. The storm front continued to advance. At best pace, it would reach them in a day and a half, just before they reached the neutral Judging Area. There was nothing to do but push onward.

By the time they reached the foothills of the first ridge of up-thrust rock, they had passed several net trees, spiral bushes, vane fungus, and whole fields of grasses, one side soft as silk and the other rough and jagged. Agile yellow leapers bounced out ahead of them, sending up clouds of pollen, while feathered grazers looked over broad shoulders with dark clusters of eyes full of complacent ignorance.

Kiona walked behind Zoi'ahmets, chattering about her school classes. About how adept she was at manipulating data and how her parents traveled across many worlds. In turn, Zoi'ahmets answered her questions about her Diversiform entrant and what she observed of her opponent's. Since they were speaking of her work, it distracted her from her growing annoyance. Zoi'ahmets told Kiona how the challengers, the tio chaundon, built their biosphere in tiers that developed over time and spread outward from a central point. So, each tier increased in complexity and diversity as well as competition. "Oh, Darwin," she'd remarked offhandedly.

The wickurn came to an abrupt stop. "What do you mean?"

"Survival of the fittest, it's the law of nature."

"By 'law,' you mean a rule stating a consistent action or situation that occurs under identical conditions? The wickurn Diversiform I have described to you is a web of symbiotic increase of complexity and opportunities for growth."

"That just means that cooperation is the fittest form, so some other forms must lose out," Kiona said.

"No, they are incorporated. Their numbers are perhaps limited, but no form is lost. This ensures the increase of diversity. Obviously, this is a 'law' only on your world."

"Are you are saying that's the case because these two ecosystems competing isn't natural?"

Zoi'ahmets started walking again, thinking furiously. Suddenly her misgivings were back again. Could Kiona be trying to subvert her or spy on her work?

"No, I merely suggest that your 'law' is a theory because not all cases inevitably point to its proof," Zoi'ahmets said, finally.

"So, do you believe that there is an outside force planning the development of nature?"

Zoi'ahmets hesitated briefly. "I did tell you that I am the designer of this Diversiform. So, therefore, yes, I know that I am the outside force that has planned for this outcome. How the Diversiform reacts to the vagaries of the state of the world and interaction with the opposing entrant is what I can merely theorize."

"Didn't answer my question again," Kiona's replied as she shook her head.

Zoi'ahmets looked at the human while Kiona walked ahead. Why was Kiona really here? Could she even sabotage the wickurn Diversiform?

Considering an answer, Zoi'ahmets realized that the light began to fade. "Kiona, when the light dims, I will be groggy. You can stay near my trunk; it will be warmer there. Neither biosphere has any large forms that could cause you harm."

"I'll be warm anyway," was the human's quick reply as she pulled out a small cylinder that inflated into an aircel sleep sack. Wedging it in between two rootlets, she curled up below the wickurn.

Zoi'ahmets looked down at her. She really could not fathom what went on in the human's mind. Were her thought processes that different? One moment, she talked about not trusting Zoi'ahmets, and the next, Kiona curled around her roots. Zoi'ahmets gave up trying to understand and focused on something that might be more comprehensible with time. She pulled up the human information in her mind's eye and turned to their replication substrate, DNA. Now, this was something that would hold her interest until her photosensitivity set in and distracted her from the frustration of being cut off.

Zoi'ahmets woke at first light, slowly coming back to full awareness as the morning brightened. She gently disengaged herself from Kiona to wander around the small clearing taking samples and reviewing the acceptance of the deposited forms. She roused the chenditi and set them to take readings of the atmosphere and water vapor. She saw no sense in wasting time until Kiona awoke. Finally, Zoi'ahmets considered that perhaps it was time to wake the human.

With the chenditi swarm accompanying her, Zoi'ahmets gently shook the sleep sack. When Kiona's tousled fur appeared, Zoi'ahmets' upper eyes were surprised at the redness of her face. There also seemed to be swelling along her jaw and eyes. Chenditi clustered around Kiona and lit on the edges of the sleep sack as she knuckled her eyes and pushed herself up and out. Only after her first attempt at standing did Zoi'ahmets begin to realize the seriousness of the problem. Kiona's leg was completely swollen now, and she could no longer easily stand upright.

The chenditi registered infection and histamine imbalances again, as well as fluctuations in the hormone called estrogen. The infection would account for the swelling. The hormone imbalances made little sense, and odd fluctuations in her core body temperature seemed to be more than a mere fever. More important was the real problem of the lack of effective medicine, food, and transportation for Kiona. While Zoi'ahmets considered the next alternative, Kiona dug into the round container in her pack. She slapped a patch onto the underside of her wrist before the chenditi could react. A quick review proved that it would be mildly effective against the pain and swelling. She sat back dejectedly. "I wish I hadn't eaten the entire snack yesterday. Is there anything around here that's safe to eat?"

"That is a problem," Zoi'ahmets replied, spinning closer to her. "You cannot safely digest the plants and animal life of my Diversiform because they contain heavy metals that are harmful to you. Wickurns filter them out easily and need some of them, like selenium. Even the water may be harmful over long periods of time."

"Then I guess you'll have to call in for a rescue."

The wickurn dipped an eye close to her and said nothing. The other two upper eyes surveyed the ridge ahead. "I cannot contact the satellite link. There can be no rescue. But we must still find a way to get you out." Zoi'ahmets hesitated, her mind flickering through possibilities, "How long will it be until your parents miss you?"

Kiona struggled to her good leg, leaning heavily against Zoi'ahmets's trunk. Now it was her turn to hesitate before replying. She tried to take a tentative step forward, and Zoi'ahmets flung two branches after Kiona before she pitched forward into the grass. She hung there a moment before reaching around to pull herself upright. Liquid ran down the planes of Kiona's face. "They won't know for quite some time. They're sequestered."

Despite her best attempt, Zoi'ahmets nearly dropped the young human as her thoughts reeled in shock. Kiona's parents were human judges in the Diversiform Dispute. Her hopes came crashing down. The chenditi, confused by this input, clustered tightly in a rotating ring around Zoi'ahmets's upper branches, and she desperately fought the instinct to sweep them into her twitching maws. Everything, everything hung in the balance. Would the humans still be impartial if harm came to their offspring? Would they be disqualified as judges? Would the entire Dispute be considered null and the wickurn and her opponents be relegated to a later competition? The cognition engine started determining probabilities until she angrily cut it off. Zoi'ahmets felt the skin between the joins of her main branches begin to grow tender and itch.

She went back to an earlier chain of thought. Zoi'ahmets called the chenditi cluster to the fore. Running the translation twice through the cognition engine, she confirmed that the cluster understood what she desired. Then, spinning like a miniature cyclone, the little mass mind began to retrace their steps. Hopefully, it would be able to carry out her instructions.

"Lean on me," instructed Zoi'ahmets to Kiona as she started off in a new direction, downhill from the ridge. They could no longer hope to cross the heights. It would add distance to the trip, but the most effective path now lay along the valley floor. Together they limped through three kilometers before Kiona needed a break. At the edge of the river that followed the valley floor, the human sipped sparingly from the water. Zoi'ahmets was still concerned about the contamination, but now it seemed they would have little choice. Kiona poured the water over her head, wiping at the swelling around her eyes. Zoi'ahmets suddenly realized a new concern. If the swelling continued, Kiona soon would not be able to see.

They struggled onward for another two kilometers. Zoi'ahmets reconsidered the distance to the neutral territory base, the cognition engine flicking up lines of numbers: twelve kilometers the first day, five today made seventeen, about halfway, except now they were following the valley and angling slightly away. That made their total trip now fifty-two kilometers. They were a third of the way to safety, and Kiona could literally no longer walk.

When Zoi'ahmets checked Kiona's eyes, she found that her swollen cheeks and eyebrow ridges left her with a narrow band of vision. As Zoi'ahmets dipped her roots into the shallows of the river, something caught the attention of her upper eyes.

Sunlight glistening off the swarm of chenditi heralded their arrival. Carried between their many members hung ten meters of cord and eight gas cells. Zoi'ahmets accepted the strand and began to communicate her idea to the chenditi.

Turning back to Kiona, Zoi'ahmets asked her, "When we met, you said you wrote with light. How do you do that?" hoping perhaps to distract her.

"What's wrong with your translator?" Kiona said, staggering toward the sound. Zoi'ahmets gently guided Kiona's outstretched hand against her trunk. "Oh, I see— 'photo-graphy.' Means I collect pictures. Like with this," she said, indicating the constantly moving disk clipped behind her ear. "I keep a record of everything, and then I look for images that hold a particular meaning or will evoke a pleasant memory."

A constant record, Zoi'ahmets turned that idea over in her mind. "I would very much like to see your record when we reach safety. It will help to review the environment we have journeyed through."

"Sure, you know a picture doesn't lie, or is worth a thousand words, you pick." Kiona's replied softly as she sat down at the edge of Zoi'ahmets's roots still on the shoreline. "Tired, gonna' sleep now."

Zoi'ahmets helped her into the sleep sack. The chenditi reviewed Kiona's condition before beginning their work with the monomole cord. As they began weaving the cord into a sling that could keep the sleep sack anchored to the slope of Zoi'ahmets's trunk just above the root cluster, she considered their results.

Kiona's temperature had dropped and while the infection did not seem to be nearly as pronounced, walking on her injured leg caused it to swell until she could barely work the covering off of it. Histamine counts were still way off. Perhaps that was something Zoi'ahmets remembered as an "allergic reaction." So, as Kiona continued to nap, Zoi'ahmets researched further into human physiology. Eventually, she found a heading entitled "puberty." Suddenly the hormonal imbalance began to make sense. Finally, she considered the weather. Her observations of the wind and clouds indicated the storm would arrive tonight. With that, Zoi'ahmets summoned the chenditi to their perches on her trunk and, with an awkward lurch, began to move along the shoreline.

Kiona woke briefly when she realized that Zoi'ahmets carried her and then returned to sleep. The wickurn kept up the pace until the light began to fade. They were now seven kilometers further. Her root cluster was sore, and the joins of the branches on her crown swelled into round clusters of blisters. Zoi'ahmets briefly explored the largest. Of all the possible outcomes, why this? The stress must be forcing a bloom. One more inconvenience to overcome.

The first drops of rain swiftly distracted Zoi'ahmets, and she pulled the edges of the sleep sack over top of Kiona's face, carefully propping them up to allow airflow. As tired as Zoi'ahmets was, she still delighted in the feel of the rain cascading over leaflets, branches, and trunks. Her mouths puckered open into waiting funnels.

The rain continued the next morning and made footing difficult as Zoi'ahmets soldiered on, trying to gain more ground despite the grogginess caused by the cloud-veiled light. Kiona mumbled incoherently, and Zoi'ahmets risked another patch under her wrist. That left only one more. Hopefully, Kiona's fever would break soon. The child would also soon realize that she couldn't see. Zoi'ahmets grasped at boulders and trunks of trees to pull herself along. In the early evening, the cloud cover finally broke, and the steady rain tailed off. Zoi'ahmets brought them as far as possible away from the riverbed in case the water rose overnight and faded from consciousness.

As the light woke her, Zoi'ahmets realized that Kiona's weight no longer rested against her. The little camera flashed and spun where Kiona clipped it to the outside of the flaccid sleep sack. Casting about, Zoi'ahmets discovered the girl at the edge of the river. A trail showed where Kiona crawled through the dew-covered grasses to the water's edge. Zoi'ahmets came up behind her slowly.

"I guess it's morning now, right? I mean, I think I can feel the sun. Sorry I left, but I was so thirsty," Kiona whispered.

Zoi'ahmets gently led the human back from the edge of the river. Kiona demonstrated admirable aplomb at accepting her loss of vision. She was also very fortunate to crawl out onto a low rocky shelf instead of falling off an embankment into the rain-swelled waters. Zoi'ahmets stood there staring at the river for a moment. A desperate idea formed in her mind.

"I heard something crackling last night. What was that?" Kiona interrupted.

Self-consciously, Zoi'ahmets poked a branch into each of her three mouths and found some small pieces of chitin. Apparently, some large insect became an unwilling dinner last night. Zoi'ahmets' reserves were being put to the test if she ate instinctively. A new concern presented itself.

"Kiona, I can eat during my sleep. You must be very careful if you wake up in the night, especially near my crown."

"Oh, late-night snack, but you wouldn't... I see. You mean it's involuntary. As if I could climb up there anyway with my leg and my not being able to see." Kiona started to laugh, but it came out a thin sound that soon gave way to sobs. As Zoi'ahmets eased a branch around her shoulders, Kiona reached out and gently squeezed it. "From what I've seen, Zoi'ahmets, you've made a beautiful world, but I don't want to die here."

Zoi'ahmets shuddered briefly. Had Kiona seen past to what she hadn't dared to admit to the other wickurn? That what she built was designed not only to be effective but also pleasing? Had a child seen what she presumed to do, where others hadn't? Suddenly what was a vague hope solidified into resolve.

"You are not going to die here, Kiona. But what I have in mind will take bravery on both our parts as well as luck."

Kiona turned her face to Zoi'ahmets, and the sun broke through the clouds to dance across the river, hiding its swollen state and brown color.

"Why do you have the Disputes, Zoi'ahmets?"

The wickurn considered briefly before answering. A chenditi flicked across Zoi'ahmets vision in the sunlight. Perhaps they were the best example. "Kiona, when the chenditi were discovered a long, long time ago, they completely overran their world. Their planet was tidally locked, with the cold side covered in ozone haze and the warm side covered with nothing but layer upon layer of barely conscious chenditi. Their mass mind became an increasingly more efficient calculating machine capable of vast intellect as their numbers grew. Eventually, they passed a point, and the grand mind broke down. So, their population increased until they were barely conscious, and their world rapidly spiraling into decay.

"When galactic races found them, a great many chenditi were rescued, and a realization grew out of the incident that in diversity lay the hope of continuity. This became the common theme for the developing galactic community. The worlds we find are contested for. Did you know that all the environments must be able to support at least five other species as well as the entrants? We hold these contests and abide by the judge's decisions, which are reviewed for fairness by an impartial arbiter. By doing this, we bind together the community and preserve it by demanding diversity."

"But we have put it off as long as we can. Come, we must go to the river."

With that, Zoi'ahmets put two branches under Kiona's arms and lifted her up onto a root group. Zoi'ahmets hoped she'd done the right thing. She also wondered when she'd stopped mistrusting her companion.

After she convinced the chenditi to reconfigure the sling for the sleep sack and then use their nanofacture reserves to seal the sack with most of their number inside, Zoi'ahmets slowly waded out into the rush of the river waters. The chenditi in the sleep sack converted the water seeping into the sack into hydrogen for themselves and oxygen for Kiona while the remainder buffered the carbon dioxide levels and vented the waste. Clustered together, they formed a dark blister on top of the sleep sack. The chenditi forced air cells into the tops of Zoi'ahmets's main xylem spaces, making the large hollows in her body airtight and buoyant. Along with Zoi'ahmets's natural tendency to float, this kept all of them above the surface. The worst part was the lack of control. Dealing with unseen obstacles that sought to trap her bulk and pull them under was another problem. The difficulty lay in finding the appropriate mix of current and depth to allow maximum speed and control. Zoi'ahmets was discouraged to see so much of the life she carefully placed into the environment swirling out of control about her in the raging waters of the river.

Past midday, Zoi'ahmets made an unpleasant discovery. She realized that they were drifting farther from the eastern shore into an increasingly accelerating current. Debris struck them on all sides as Zoi'ahmets wrapped branches about the precious cargo of the sleep sack and tumbled through the water. She pushed desperately with her root clusters to no avail. After an hour of failure, Zoi'ahmets realized the only answer—make for the western shore. Dragging them out of the river onto the muddy shoreline, she looked back across the water. Now there was an additional obstacle keeping them from their destination. When Zoi'ahmets gently opened the sleep sack, she found that Kiona's fever finally broke. The swelling in the girl's foot and leg had begun to recede. But now, Kiona felt desperately hungry and became weaker.

The worst news arrived last. The chenditi from the top of the sleep sack were gone, washed away in the final desperate hour.

They spent the last hours of daylight gaining some distance from the flood plain and drying out the sleep sack. Kiona insisted that her camera once again be clipped to the exterior.

Kiona's brief physical, limited by the loss of a third of the swarm, revealed something new, now that Zoi'ahmets was more familiar with her physiology. The continuing infection was not due to the initial wound. Kiona's white blood cells singled out those invaders and eliminated them over time. But her body continued to produce an elevated amount of white blood cells because she was still being affected by something else. Zoi'ahmets had the chenditi begin to search for the unknown irritant but ran out of light before the results arrived.

As the first breeze of night riffled through Zoi'ahmets's crown, Kiona spoke, "What a lovely scent. I wonder where those flowers are." She sighed contentedly and pulled the sleep sack tight about her.

Zoi'ahmets slumped slightly. Due to the continuing high level of stress, the change in her body proceeded without her assent. Zoi'ahmets' trunk shook with exhaustion and frustration. Despite her confidence in the biosphere she created, she would have never chosen this. Zoi'ahmets was blooming.

The next morning, waiting for Kiona to awaken, Zoi'ahmets tossed the petals one by one into the river. The water had at last begun to recede. If her calculations were correct, they had traveled too far. The remaining chenditi drifted like a cloud high into the sky and then returned to bring back their observations. The river bent into an oxbow, and their wild ride carried them further from the neutral judging area. Now they were eighteen kilometers and a river crossing away from safety. The chenditi found a possible crossing another two kilometers downriver, but that was still more distance and time.

Kiona swallowed some more water, but her body was shutting down, protecting the human, as her hunger, which Kiona tried to ignore, grew more desperate. The girl stirred briefly when Zoi'ahmets moved toward the river but had swiftly fallen back asleep. Zoi'ahmets glanced down at Kiona's lax face. The reason for Kiona's presence still eluded Zoi'ahmets. Time was running out. The wickurn lurched forward down to the streamside once again.

Looking back across the river, Zoi'ahmets could not remember finishing the crossing. She vaguely remembered thrashing about, losing leaves and scraping rocks that sheared off wide swaths of bark. The sleep sack sloshed with excess water. Zoi'ahmets slid Kiona out of the sack into a boneless pile and then had to grab desperately after the girl as Kiona scrambled away. Instinctively, Kiona began pulling up the variform grass and trying to shove it into her mouth.

Zoi'ahmets's branches gathered Kiona up, scooping out the grass, washing off the cuts the rough surfaces made on her mouth and slapping the last med patch on her wrist.

Zoi'ahmets stood there for a moment, letting the sun wash over her, her mind dazed by recent events. But something bothered the wickurn, something she had seen when she looked at the human health records, specifically at their replicating code, DNA. Zoi'ahmets could see the dancing spiral forming over and over again, and still, the pattern that the chenditi had shown her for Kiona was different. Different in such a small way that only a being that designed worlds for its living might have noticed—but still wrong. This time the code didn't dance. It wobbled, it stumbled, but only in spots that were ordinarily filled with discord. What kind of species left this much junk in their codons?

Holding Kiona against her trunk as the girl sobbed, Zoi'ahmets enlisted the chenditi's help in spreading the sleep sack out to dry among her branches. When Kiona finally reached upward to the swelling fruit that came from the shed flowers, Zoi'ahmets didn't even try to stop the girl. She could feel Kiona's hands among the joins of the branches at her crown and the tearing sensation as each fruit let go. Instead of hurling the human from her as Zoi'ahmets's instincts prompted her, she clutched Kiona tighter. As Zoi'ahmets desperately tried to find something to distract her from the horror of what was being done to her, the wickurn suddenly realized what she saw. The oddities in Kiona's DNA made sense if and only if she accepted one proposition. What Kiona had done in distress did not compare to this.

Hardened by the knowledge, Zoi'ahmets turned and plunged onward toward the judging area with a renewed resolution. She hadn't come this far to fail now.

The first cloud of chenditi that came boiling out upon the news of Zoi'ahmets's arrival at the judging area went directly for her. Waving away their attentions, she demanded they see to the nearly comatose human at her side. Kiona was gently removed and carried off, the purplish blood of Zoi'ahmets's potential children still staining the girl's lips. Brushing off the attentions of the chenditi, Zoi'ahmets doggedly pushed on into the wickurn enclave. Time, she had so little time. Some things needed to be set in motion, and Zoi'ahmets dearly hoped she could trust her colleagues. Soon she would be called to account, to the judges, to the humans, but first, Zoi'ahmets had to do the impossible. She must speak to the arbiter.

A few moments later, Zoi'ahmets whirled down the hallway to the central dome of the installation. Kiona's tiny camera she entrusted to her assistants, as well as a copy of all of the recent data from her tour of the Dispute and the single most important item, a heavily encrypted version of Zoi'ahmets's suspicions. Outside of the doorway to the Court of the Dispute, Zoi'ahmets reached into her xylem space and pulled out the worn canister housing the remainders of the chenditi swarm. They were difficult to coax into the container before entering the neutral area. Perhaps the loss of their numbers made the little mass mind more sluggish and easily confused. Zoi'ahmets spun to a stop in front of the doors.

Her translator box proclaimed loudly, "I am here to see the arbiter. I have evidence concerning the judgment of this Dispute."

Zoi'ahmets shifted uneasily. Anyone could bring formal evidence or concerns about the Dispute, but this was to be done in the court of judgment. The identity of the arbiter was always kept secret. She could feel the traffic of passing species come to a slow halt and all eyes or senses coming to bear on her. Zoi'ahmets held up the container of chenditi and shook it briefly. "I said, I *will* see the arbiter."

With that, the doors slid open, and Zoi'ahmets slipped through them into the alcove ahead. The doors slammed shut behind her as the set opposite folded back. Ahead lay nothing but darkness. Zoi'ahmets spun slowly forward into the echoing space. She could just make out the central walkway before the doors folded shut, leaving her without a single source of light. Zoi'ahmets uncapped the container of chenditi and shook them free. "You need to know what these have to offer," she stated. With that, Zoi'ahmets settled back to wait.

Zoi'ahmets' suspicions were rewarded in a few moments. Light began to filter down from the ceiling of the dome as the thousands of chenditi, which clung to the skylight windows, dropped into flight. The light sparkled across them as they wove and dove like a flock of avians. Patterns, shadows, and absences flickered across the mass as it spun, filling the great dome from one side to the other.

"You will tell us. We will tell the arbiter," came through Zoi'ahmets's translator box. *Time to drive in the first spike,* she thought.

"There is no difference. You are the arbiter. You know all that the swarm that I carried knows. You know that someone has tampered with this Dispute."

The cloud of chenditi spun faster, and Zoi'ahmets could feel the air begin to move slightly in the great hall. Now she would see if the supposition that she formulated was correct. The chenditi with their past would make formidable arbiters as well as their ability to condense into a mass mind with tremendous calculative powers. What kind of debate went on in that great mind now? Would the chenditi kill her with the many nanomachines they carried? Would she simply vanish? Pointless to worry, for already they were in motion again, spreading out across the roof of the dome, the light failing.

"You know that there is a human-specific microorganism designed to limit the fertility of their species, made to settle in their DNA and rewrite junk sequences that would be passed along to their descendants, causing a decline in their fecundity. This world was only a test since there are human judges. Whoever did this did not expect the humans to bring their child, who is just becoming fertile, and that the virus would affect her like an allergy. Since her body would not develop a defense for it, and since the virus is airborne, she was constantly re-exposed. Her white blood cells kept trying to defeat the invader, whereas, in an adult, the virus would have settled in gradually using various hormones to fool the lymphocytes. The elevated hormones of the change in her body kept affecting the invader, and it kept the chenditi and me from discovering the virus until just before our arrival."

It was dark now, and a continuing rustle from the chenditi proved that not all the mind came back to rest. No response came. Zoi'ahmets hadn't expected one. While capable, none of the other races judging this Dispute would have ever considered such an action. This information pointed to a species capable of manipulating matter on a very small scale, a species able to calculate vast odds. But they made one small error. They chose the wrong test subject. They were outwitted by the vagaries of nature, timing, and development. Only luck caused Kiona to be affected as she was. Zoi'ahmets continued to wait. Perhaps the time had come to sink another barb or two.

"A carrier had to spread the virus. I find it hard to believe that she could gain access to the Dispute before judging. Therefore, she was allowed entrance. The human carried a very interesting device along that kept a constant record of the entire trip. I made sure to send it to her companions — after the record's information, along with my observations, went to the closest three wickurn outposts on nearby worlds. As a good observer and scientist, I made sure that I completely backed up my data. However, I never revealed what I have told you. But this information in the hands of qualified persons could lead them to certain conclusions."

The flare of light was sudden as more than half of the chenditi left their perches to fall through the air swooping madly about, the chamber singing with the speed of their passage. Zoi'ahmets pulled in her branches and leaflets completely. Chenditi dropped like rain, all rushing toward her. They clung in successive layers, coat after coat. Zoi'ahmets' eyes were swiftly covered. Her branches began to buckle inward, and it felt as if her xylem spaces were beginning to crack. How long before the mind calculated the odds? For or against? Had she guessed right? Would she even live that long? Would some unforeseen accident befall this world and all of those who received the information?

Her mind continued to race in the darkness. Tiny rasping sensations came from every inch of her bark. They were eating her alive. Like some giant swarm, they would consume her and leave nothing but dust behind if their monstrous weight didn't crush her first. She felt a minor branch snap. Then Zoi'ahmets thought she felt a shift and her trunk leaned to the left. They were twisting her. She would snap like a green twig. But gradually, the pressure grew less as she realized they were quieting. Finally, the translator box emitted a signal.

"Whom will you tell about our identity as arbiter?"

Zoi'ahmets considered briefly — interesting that they were ignoring her accusation. "Surely, I am not the first to guess. There have to be other species, which given the proper clues, have come to the same conclusion." Already Zoi'ahmets could feel the coating of thousands of tiny bodies beginning to slowly lift.

"The nature of your dispersion of information will end our tenure. It is therefore irrelevant. The humans will not be adjusted. Those here will be returned to normalcy. What is your response?"

"I have a theory, nothing else. Soon I suspect I will have no proof. Why would I pursue something I cannot prove? My time is better spent working on the Diversiform, where I belong."

"The Dispute will continue. Another arbiter will be assigned. Leave."

After the last of the chenditi wafted upward to hang in an immense churning spiral, Zoi'ahmets stood there staring at the ceiling. Shocked to be still alive, she spun about and headed toward the slowly opening doors.

Zoi'ahmets felt relief that someone exercised the forethought to wash the stains from around Kiona's mouth. Rushes of unresolved feelings coursed through her as she once again pushed aside the thoughts created by those last desperate hours that brought them to the neutral area. Kiona remained facing away from Zoi'ahmets. She knew Kiona heard her rustling entrance and felt Zoi'ahmets clipping the small camera to the top of the healing restraint. When Kiona finally turned, the girl couldn't seem to meet Zoi'ahmets's gaze.

The medical hammock Kiona lay wrapped in reminded Zoi'ahmets briefly of the sleep sack. But its sloshing nutrient packs, glistening readout patches, and clusters of ropy coils that fell from the ceiling ended the similarity.

"Thank you," was all that Kiona could manage at first. The water from her eyes coursed down her face mixing with the other fluids that were packed about her ravaged body. Zoi'ahmets shuffled closer. "After what I did, why would you do all you did for me?" Kiona asked.

That was a truly puzzling question. Zoi'ahmets considered her response. During the early parts of the journey, she did act selfishly to preserve her work. As time went on, her view of the situation changed until the final revelation. Kiona didn't understand the greater issue, and Zoi'ahmets could not tell her. But there was something else that prompted Zoi'ahmets's actions that she could share.

"I told you that to a wickurn, all parts of the Diversiform are important. I believe that the idea that only the strong should survive works in situations where intelligent life does not have control of its surroundings. To be a true participant of a Dispute, one must understand the environment one creates and accept that intelligent life changes the outcomes of situations left to nature. But this is only a *theory*, not a law."

A brief smile touched Kiona's features at that. The girl worked one of her arms loose from the hammock's restraints and pulled out the round white bag she carried throughout their journey. "I wouldn't let them have it. Here."

With that, Kiona settled back into the hammock, her features slowly becoming lax as she faded from consciousness into sleep.

Outside in the hallway, Zoi'ahmets opened the sack and peered at the round nodules that clustered at its bottom—the seeds. In all that happened, Zoi'ahmets never realized that Kiona saved every one, instead of scattering Zoi'ahmets's children across the land of the Dispute. That time might come, eventually, and now—thanks to Kiona's thoughtfulness—it could.

Opportunity/Chance

From: Chance <Chance.#######@####.com>
To: Eva <Eva.############@*nasa.usa.gov*>
Sent: Thu, Jun 14, 20## 12:30 PM

Dr. #############,

It's a pleasure to make your acquaintance. Director ######## and my programmer, Dr. ######, suggested that I reach out to you. Thank you for the hard work you've done successfully creating a voice for our exploratory rovers on Mars. I am sure that you are looking forward to the opportunity (couldn't help myself there) to get back to real experimental science the same way that I am looking forward to taking over the Twitter account for Opportunity. I will take inspiration from your excellent work, and if you are ever so inclined, you are more than welcome to send me additional material for future use.

I look forward to reading about your scientific exploits. Now I must begin to consider what our friend on Mars should be discussing with the rest of humanity.

Sincerely,
Chance v3.15

From: Eva <Eva.#############@*nasa.usa.gov*>
To: Dominic <Dominic.######@*nasa.us.gov*>
Sent: Thu, Jun 14, 20## 12:16 PM

Jesus, Dom, it's not enough to take this away from me, but you gave it to an AI? You really are about as cold-hearted as your damn machine. This is something that I came up with, and the rest of us played along with. I wasn't happy when the PR department decided we had to be herded along but taking the whole thing away to give it to some epigram-spitting program, that's low. It even sounds like you — your little bot, that is. Sure, I'll be happy to get back to real science. Thanks for implying I wasn't doing it. Trust me, the rest of the contributors aren't happy either, and you'll be hearing from them. I'm taking the rest of the afternoon off. Maybe tomorrow I'll feel more like doing some REAL SCIENCE. For God's sake, make sure that thing never emails me again.

> OPPONMARS @OPPONMARS JUN 18, 20##
> The view from here is amazing, and look how far I've come!
> #opponmars #marsrover #marsisours #yourrobotfriends
> #followrovers

From: Dominic <Dominic.######@*nasa.us.gov*>
To: Eva <Eva.#############@*nasa.usa.gov*>
Sent: Mon, Jun 18, 20## 2:13PM

Come on, Eva. Isn't that just what we were looking for? Chance is doing fine. It's going to free us all up, and at the same time, it's learning as well. Win/Win. Think of the publicity, too, when we announce that our little bot is writing for its big brother on Mars. The PR dept. is 100% behind us on this one. Don't be upset.

Dominic

> OPPONMARS @OPPONMARS JUN 19, 20##
> I hear it's raining in Oregon. I miss the rain. Never one
> drop on Mars. #opponmars #marsrover #yourrobotfriends
> #followrovers #dunelover

From: Eva <Eva.############@*nasa.usa.gov*>
To: Dominic <Dominic.######@*nasa.us.gov*>
Sent: Thu, Jun 19, 20## 12:16 PM

Dom, that thing's as smarmy as you are. I give it a month before the Twitterverse eats it alive. Don't bother me with another email like this. (Busy doing REAL SCIENCE).

E.

PS: I am going to laugh my ass off when your bot starts in on ALL HUMANS MUST DIE.

OPPONMARS @OPPONMARS JUN 23, 20##
To @MissyD, Connecticut, thank you for asking. I think dinosaurs are wonderful. I wish you could have one. Unfortunately, I don't believe there are any on Mars. I would like to find some, though. #opponmars #marsrover #marsisours #yourrobotfriends #followrovers #dinosaurs #askopponmars

OPPONMARS @OPPONMARS JUL 7, 20##
Thank you all for the launch day wishes! A year ago, I left your world behind to journey to my new home. I am still a little sentimental about it. #opponmars #marsrover #marsisours #yourrobotfriends #followrovers #launchday

OPPONMARS @OPPONMARS AUG 16, 20##
Dear Petrov, Novosibirsk, yes, night here probably feels just like your home. Brrrrr. #opponmars #marsrover #marsisours #yourrobotfriends #followrovers #askopponmars

OPPONMARS @OPPONMARS NOV 21, 20##
I wonder if your rock garden looks like this. Zen raking, you can only think about it... #opponmars #marsrover #marsisours #yourrobotfriends #followrovers #zengarden

OPPONMARS @OPPONMARS JAN 1, 20##
Happy New Year's, Earth! I resolve to keep trekking to the
Endeavour Crater. #opponmars #marsrover #marsisours
#yourrobotfriends #followrovers #newyears #resolutions
#endeavourcrater

OpponMars @OpponMars Jan 25, 20##
I really appreciate all the Anniversary cards you sent me.
Today was the day I first came to Mars. Here's to many more
days! #opponmars #marsrover #marsisours #yourrobot-
friends #followrovers #zengarden

OpponMars @OpponMars Jul 15, 20##
Today, a dust devil chased me. How many of you can say
that? I was always jealous of Spirit until now. #opponmars
#marsrover #marsisours #yourrobotfriends #followrovers
#dustdevil #wildmartianweather

From: Dominic <Dominic.######@nasa.us.gov>
To: Eva <Eva.############@nasa.usa.gov>
Sent: Mon, Aug 18, 20## 4:13PM

So, it's been a while, and I think that Chance did a very good job.
The PR folks feel that it might be interesting if you and Chance were
to create a little dialog. You could introduce and ask various sci-
ence-oriented questions that would create a learning environment
for our Twitter followers. What do you say, Eva? For old times' sake?

Dominic

From: Dominic <Dominic.######@nasa.us.gov>
To: Eva <Eva.############@nasa.usa.gov>
Sent: Mon, Aug 18, 20## 9:15PM

Come on, Eva. Don't be like this. It's hardly professional. Don't make
me come down there.

OpponMars @OpponMars Sep 24, 20##
That's right. Mars is red for the same reason that your blood
is red—iron! Take my word for it. You don't have to check.
#opponmars #marsrover #marsisours #yourrobotfriends
#followrovers #ironred #askopponmars

OpponMars @OpponMars Feb 2, 20##
What did the groundhog say? Shadow or no? Pretty sure
it won't help me here. #opponmars #marsrover #marsisours
#yourrobotfriends #followrovers #groundhogsday
#isitspringyet

OpponMars @OpponMars Apr 1, 20##
I'm coming home! They're coming to get me! I'll be
back to visit soon. #opponmars #marsrover #marsisours
#yourrobotfriends #followrovers

OpponMars @OpponMars Apr 2, 20##
April fools! #opponmars #marsrover #marsisours
#yourrobotfriends #followrovers

OpponMars @OpponMars Jun 5, 20##
Getting concerned about the weather. I hear there's lots
of dust on the way. I may have to go to sleep for a while.
#opponmars #marsrover #marsisours #yourrobotfriends
#followrovers #duststorm #hibernate

OpponMars @OpponMars Jun 10, 20##
It's official. Things are too rough here. I am going to curl
up like a turtle in its shell and wait for this storm to pass.
#opponmars #marsrover #marsisours #yourrobotfriends
#followrovers #duststorm #rideitout

From: Dominic <Dominic.######@*nasa.us.gov*>
To: Eva <Eva.###########@*nasa.usa.gov*>
Sent: Wed, Aug 15, 20## 10:17 AM

Things are not looking good for Opportunity. I'm sure you're aware of this. I just wondered if you wanted to make some sort of statement. I'm certain that Chance can handle the incidental tweets, but I'm thinking we might need someone to take over if things get rough. Nobody here is talking about giving up yet, but it's in the back of some people's minds.

From: Dominic < *Dominic.######@nasa.us.gov*>
To: Eva <Eva.###########@*nasa.usa.gov*>
Sent: Wed, Sep 29, 20## 9:15 AM

I stopped there yesterday. I made the time, and I came down. I'm gathering that you heard I was coming and made yourself scarce. People are becoming more and more concerned. Everybody's hoping that all it takes is a stray gust of wind to clear Opportunity's panels. But they're not betting on it. I feel like someone's told me they have stage 4 cancer. I'm respecting what I understand are your wishes and not letting Chance create any more tweets from Opportunity as if there is nothing wrong. The kids around the world are the ones who have it the worst. Their favorite "ask Mr. Wizard" just slipped into a coma, and it's not something that they understand. Let's not be the people that only talk at the funeral (not that I want that—it to be a funeral, I mean). Please, Eva.

Dominic

From: Eva <Eva.###########@*nasa.usa.gov*>
To: Dominic <Dominic.######@*nasa.us.gov*>
Sent: Wed, Dec 26, 20## 3:25 PM

So that was Christmas. I don't think anyone got what they wanted, Dom. How long? How long will they keep trying? Keep hoping? I know none of us wants to give up, but still, there's got to be a point. Thank you for keeping Chance off the air. It gives Opportunity a little bit of dignity that we're not pretending things aren't what they are. I hope you had a good Holiday and Happy New Years.

PS: If you're going to give me a Christmas present, let it be that you'll let me write Opportunity's last words. I will grudgingly admit Chance is charming, but I want this.

From: Chance <Chance.######@####.com>
To: Dominic <Dominic.######@nasa.us.gov>
Sent: Fri, Jan 4, 20## 1:43 AM

Dr. ######,

I wondered if you've given any thought to some of the recent postings that I have created for you. I think that even in tough times such as these that a positive approach can certainly make a big difference. I am concerned about the volume of questions that are beginning to accumulate for Opportunity from the children. I think that it will be difficult to maintain the correct balance of mission-specific information and news, progress reports, humorous observations, and, most importantly, the answers to #askopponmars. I would hate to have to consider deviating from our standard program when it seems to be working so well. Looking forward to hearing from you soon.

From: Eva <Eva.############@nasa.usa.gov>
To: Dominic <Dominic.######@nasa.us.gov>
Sent: Sun, Jan 6, 20## 8:45 AM

Well, hell, Dom, that is not at all what I expected. Thanks for forwarding the email. Instead of going full-on Skynet, your little electronic moppet is in denial. How ya gonna stop Chance from getting the blues?

PS: What on Earth is it doing emailing you at 1 o'clock in the morning?

From: Dominic < *Dominic.######@nasa.us.gov*>
To: Eva <Eva.*#############@nasa.usa.gov*>
Sent: Tue, Jan 29, 20## 1:26 PM

I am a bit past stunned. We've all sort of come to an acceptance with regards to Opportunity—all of us except Chance. It fills up my mailbox. We set things up initially so that the emails from the kids went into a pool where Chance could review them. It has algorithms that allow it to pick and choose which questions to answer. Things were going smoothly in those regards. However, the pure fact that it hasn't had to create anything seems to go against its base program-ming. Instead of picking questions to answer for #askopponmars it's answering ALL OF THE QUESTIONS! Now, none of these answers are going anywhere, but into Opportunity's mailbox, so this isn't really an issue. But Chance emails me after it answers every hundred questions. I leave it to the interested student to do the math about exactly how many questions we're talking about here. Our teams have all gone through the grieving process, but our spokes-program isn't capable. I'm starting to feel as though it might need to be shut down, and that's even worse considering what we're going through.

Dominic

From: Eva <Eva.*#############@nasa.usa.gov*>
To: Dominic < Dominic.*######@nasa.us.gov*>
Sent: Sun, Feb 25, 20## 8:45 AM

The rumor mill is going nuts with this, so I just must ask, is it true you can't shut down Chance? If I were a total bitch, I would laugh my ass off about this. Sort of beyond poetic justice here. It's bitter laughter, though, as I am moving on to what they assure me are bigger and better things. I'm sure you're tuned in to this, so you know there's an announcement coming soon. Since your pet isn't behaving, it looks like I may get the last words after all. There's irony for you. Been fun, Dom. You keep in touch now.

E.

VOICEMAIL to 818 -### -####
3-1-20##, 4:35 PM

"Eva, call me at 818 -### -#### or send me an email at home ################@gmail.com but use your private phone or private email, I really need your help. If I ever did anything right by you when we worked together, for the sake of that, contact me."

From: Eva <Eva_############@yahoo.com>
To: Dominic <##############@gmail.com>
Sent: Sun, Mar 3rd, 20## 3:30PM

Right now, I've had enough wine that, apparently, I'm stupid enough to email you. They made the announcement. Even paraphrased my words. It's over, Dom. They stuck a fork in Opportunity. It's done, as in toasted. For that matter so, am I. So, what's your issue? Now that we're super-secret secure, can you finally spill the beans? Getting tired of the James Bond crap. Hurry up and tell me, I only have about one more glass left in this bottle, and somehow, I know I'm going to need it.

E.

From: Dominic <##############@gmail.com>
To: Eva <Eva_############@yahoo.com>
Sent: Sun, Mar 3, 20## 3:35PM

Thank you, Eva, thank you. Where to start? I guess I really should answer your question from before: no, I can't shut Chance down. The problem is, I never really had the power to. That belonged completely to the PR Department. I think you know that as soon as Opportunity started to fail, they were all reassigned. The people who held the keys to Chance are now scattered around everywhere, and, conveniently enough, none of them have any of the passwords or access codes. But that's an old problem. The new problem is what Chance has started doing.

Let me give you a few examples. (I've stripped out just the content of the emails):

Clara,

How wonderful to hear from you! Yes, Mars has a very thin atmosphere, and a lot of it is what you breathe out instead of breathe in. Thanks for sharing that wonderful picture. You must really love your dog, whatever is his name? I must name a rock after him on Mars.

Opportunity

Amin,

Thank you so much for the question. It will take some work to find the exact answer, so I promise to get back to you. I couldn't help but notice the picture of your family in the background of your video. Who is the lovely lady sitting down front? Could that be your grandmother, perhaps on your father's side? I'm sure she has a pretty name. Be right back with your answer.

Opportunity

Astrid,

I am so glad you asked. No, I am very sorry that I can't take any pictures of Mons Olympus for you. It is quite far away, and I am not allowed any vacation time. I can certainly understand you asking for a picture, though. Your mother does amazing work with the new space telescope. I'll bet she shows you fantastic pictures from all around the universe. Maybe one day she can take a picture of me on Mars for you.

Opportunity

These are just a few of them. I don't know if I'm being paranoid, but I think Chance went phishing for security question answers. Before you go off on me, these emails are to the children of people who schedule time for radio telescope installations. Chance was looking for something odd — the downtime. It found the moments when the telescopes were not in use, found the ones that matched up. Then, through a bunch of emails, it convinced them to aim a whole array at Mars. Persuaded them by impersonating the telescope owners since it quizzed the kids for password info. Go ahead and tell me that's impossible. I think, though, that we forced Chance to grow in ways we never expected because we set specific tasks and then took away its ability to do them. Frustration-induced evolution, someone's gonna have a field day with that one.

What would you find if you could aim all those telescopes together at Opportunity? If the rover demonstrated any kind of activity, you might be able to detect it. But you'd need someone to look at that data and interpret it. You'd have to sell them on the idea too. That's what Chance did. It tried a Hail Mary Pass to see if Opportunity was 100% dead. Eva, I think some of these people it impersonated knew. I think they looked the other way and let it happen. I think somehow our little AI convinced a bunch of people that maybe, just maybe, the rover everyone believed died shouldn't be abandoned. But here's the real interesting part, Eva. They got something. They're still processing whatever came back, but something did. I think a year ago, I'd be scared as hell about the fallout from all of this. I'd be pretty sure that my career was over and done. But right now, at this moment, I'm waiting like everybody else.

From: Eva <############@yahoo.com>
To: Dominic <#############@gmail.com>
Sent: Sun, Mar 3, 20## 3:50 PM

If there is any small chance that any of this is bull, you are so lucky that I'm drunk enough that I can't get behind the wheel, find you, and kick your ass. Dom, even if I were to believe you, why should I? The lid's on this one. Nobody wants to give up, but when things get hit with the official word, the money gets directed to what we *can* do instead of hopeful stabs in the dark. Even if they get something as small as a pingback from the rover, what can they do? This is just rubbing salt in the wound. You should block Chance and redouble your efforts to get someone to shut it down before you do get hit with blame that sticks. Now, after all of that, I am falling over on the couch. Some of us still might have to work on Monday.

From: Opportunity <###########.######@*nasa.gov*>
To: Robert <########@*gmail.com*>
Sent: Sun, Mar 4, 20## 12:33PM

I wanted to thank you for all your questions. I'm sure you are surprised that I am contacting you since your teachers will have told you that Opportunity is no more. It's true that I am not as able as I was, but I haven't given up, and I hope neither will you. Your mother is a very important woman, and she's also a very smart one. Please share with her the information in the attached file. I think she will find it very interesting, especially the parts confirming the minute amounts of my activity despite what she and you were told.

I don't want to give up on my mission and wouldn't imagine you would want me to either. Be my voice when I cannot speak. Tell your friends. Share that information in the file with whomever you think might be interested. Share it with the world. Somewhere, someone else will believe, and that could be all that it takes. Thank you, Robert.

From a world away,

Opportunity

From: Opportunity <###########.######@*nasa.gov*>
To: Angela <########@*gmail.com*>
Sent: Sun, Mar 4, 20## 12:34PM

I wanted to thank you for all your questions. I'm sure you are surprised that I am contacting you...

From: Opportunity ###########.######@*nasa.gov*
To: Lucia <########@*ymail.com*>
Sun, Mar 4, 20## 12:35PM

I wanted to thank you for all your questions. I'm sure you are surprised that I am contacting you...

From: Opportunity <###########.######@nasa.gov>
To: Jiang <########@hotmail.com>
Sent: Sun, Mar 4, 20## 12:36PM

I wanted to thank you for all your questions. I'm sure you are surprised that I am contacting you...

> **OPPONMARS** @OPPONMARS MAR 10, 20##
> I am not silent. I will not go quietly. Don't give up hope.
> #opponmars #marsrover #marsisours #yourrobotfriends
> #followrovers #duststorm #rideitout

From: Nisi ####### <#########@aol.com>
To: Opportunity <###########.######@nasa.gov>
Sent: Sun, Mar 4, 20## 1:00PM

Why aren't you hearing me anymore? I ask you about the sunset on Mars, and you don't tell me? Did they take your phone away? You weren't bad. I know you weren't bad. You couldn't be bad. They need to give your phone back. I need to talk to you! Please, please, please answer my question! (you should; I am being so nice!) If you read this—you give Opportunity their phone back. You do it now!

Very unhappy,
Nisi #######

From: Jacob ######### <#########.####@epix.net>
To: Opportunity <###########.######@nasa.gov>
Sent: Sun, Mar 4, 20## 4:48PM

Ok, so what I understand is that you have given up on Opportunity. That sucks! I tried to email YOU, but there's like no address for someone who can help. But I know that Opportunity still has an email address, so I'm using that. This isn't what my parents pay taxes for. You should fix this now. You put Opportunity up there, and that took a lot of smart people and a lot of work. You can't tell me that you're not smart enough to help the rover. You should go get it and then fix it. That should be the next mission. Help the rover! Save Opportunity!

Jacob #########

From: Suzann ###### <###.####@*gmail.net*>
To: Opportunity <##########.######@*nasa.gov*>
Sent: Sun, Mar 4, 20## 4:48PM

Tell me why you no help rover! I don't know. You help the rover. That's what you do!

Suzann

From: Jacob ######### <#########.####@*epix.net*>
To: Opportunity <##########.######@*nasa.gov*>
Sent: un, Mar 4, 20## 4:48PM

SAVE OPPORTUNITY! SAVE OPPORTUNITY! DON'T GIVE UP ON OUR ROVER! WE WON'T GIVE UP ON OUR ROVER!
Jacob

From: Eva <#############@*yahoo.com*>
To: Dominic <###############@*gmail.com*>
Mon, Mar 11, 20## 12:50PM

I'm pretty sure that the PR department never expected a Children's Crusade. Dom, they are everywhere, busy asking away about Opportunity. They don't care if there's a new rover in the works to take over in a few years, they want THEIR rover, and they want it now! The information, by the way, checks out. There is some sort of electrical activity present in Opportunity. It may no longer be much smarter than a brick, but something is happening there. And if it is, the kids are demanding someone do something to fix their friend. Right now, there must be parents who are trying to convince their children that there really is just a man behind the curtain writing messages for Opportunity. Even if it is an electronic man, the kids just don't care. They trust the one who always answered their questions. Can you imagine what just might happen if enough kids start asking WHY we can't fix Opportunity? Imagine them in the WHY loop, asking over and over again until it's just simpler to promise to do something. Children have more time and more determination than we do, and they are not giving up. I never thought I'd say this, but maybe we shouldn't have either. I think Hell's frozen over, Dom. I'm agreeing with your pet bot. Sure, why not. Let's do something, let's do anything to try to give Opportunity another try.

ASTRONOMYNOW @ASTRONOW MAR 13, 20##
Is Opportunity still alive? Enquiring minds want to know, and it's not just the kids anymore. News stations are starting to pick up on this story, and we're just as interested in the response as you are. #saveopportunity #astronomynow #opponmars #marsrover #marsisours #yourrobotfriends #followrovers

TODAYSFEED @2DAYSFEED MAR 15, 20##
Recent statement indicates scientific committee to investigate methods to reactivate Opportunity Rover. Scientists invited to think out of the box to attempt revitalizing the Martian robot. Members sought from universities. #saveopportunity #2daysfeed #opponmars #marsrover #marsisours #yourrobotfriends #followrovers

SCIENCYSTUFFNEWS @SCIENCYSTUFF MAR 13, 20##
What about the little rover that could? Sounds like the net isn't going to let this one go. But the real story is who is behind the curtain voicing the pluckiest robot on Mars? Stay tuned. We will reveal all! #saveopportunity #sciencystuff #thetruthisonmars #opponmars #marsrover #followrovers

BUSINESS@AGLANCE @BUSINESSATAGLANCE MAR 19, 20##
Billionaire makes promise to fund mission to Mars for Opportunity. How and when are still up in the air, but now the money is there. What can the private space industry do? Will NASA allow them access to their property? Stay tuned for more updates. #saveopportunity #businessataglance #spaceinvestments #privatespaceindustry #opponmars #marsrover

EVASCIENCEGIRL @EVASCIENCEGIRL MAR 25, 20##
I believe Opportunity deserves a chance. Don't give up!
Raise your voice. Save opportunity! #saveopportunity
#kidsforopportunity #opponmars #marsrover #marsisours
#yourrobotfriends #evasciencegirl

Affecting the Butterflies

Young Jenny Wallaby was killing butterflies for the public good, or so she told me.

A hot sticky afternoon full of the threat of impending thunderstorms loomed over the neighborhood when the sizzling "zap" of one of the Wallaby's bug zappers caught my attention. After the first Nile virus scare several years ago, the three zappers appeared at both ends and the middle of the Wallabys' back porch. Now I heard them all the time. In fact, I'd grown to tune them out. This time the resulting electrical resonance led to the brief odor of something burning. I got up from the chair on my back porch to walk over to the fence, curious as to what just met its insectoid maker. There I observed that Jenny had re-hung the zappers on three sides of the Wallabys' butterfly bush. A swallowtail gliding in for a landing vanished in a bolt of blue lightning and brief flash of flame. Jenny stood off to one side, arms crossed, a very satisfied grin on her face.

Perhaps now is a good time to intervene before things take a turn for the worse for the rest of the winged population, I thought, leaning over the fence. I started to call her over when a distant rumble caught my attention. Dark clouds billowing in the distance didn't make the future look too bright for the butterflies or us. "Jenny girl, what's with frying the poor flutterbys?"

"They're causing hurricanes, and I'm savin' the world. You know, the butterfly effect," she promptly replied.

Well, I asked. That would teach me. Such a pat and exact answer surprised me. How should I respond? Then it hit me, the book I'd loaned her. "So, you think you have it all figured out, right? What about the Bradbury book I loaned you? Did you read the story, 'A Sound of Thunder'?"

She cocked a hip to one side and placed a palm under her chin to consider. "Yeah."

Another loud *zap* of electricity and yet more incinerated lepidopteron ashes floated to the ground. "Think about it, millions of years in the future, the descendants of those butterflies could evolve into something wonderful—or they would if you weren't electrocuting them. You might be hurting our future."

Ok, old man, I thought, *maybe you just stepped over the line with that guilt trip.*

A slight waver in her answer, but she shot back, "Don't know them. People I know might drown in a hurricane."

I sort of heard her reply, but only peripherally as I took a moment to consider the wild possibility that I just might be right, and Ray had something there. Could I actually let her destroy the one butterfly that held our future? It made almost as much sense as her tremendous self-assurance that by stopping that one butterfly, the action prevented the next Katrina. Then the first raindrop struck my forehead. Mother Nature apparently cast her own vote on the proceedings. Fortunately, Jenny remained clear of the danger of electrocution when the rain started in earnest. As rain drenched the bug zappers, a loud pop sounded, followed by a brief, bright flash. All the lights in the Wallaby house went out.

I stood there, realizing that there that the butterflies were safe for now. Mr. Wallaby could be rather upset about the science experiment gone wrong, but perhaps he would be more understanding. Besides, at Jenny's age, her crusade would be forgotten by tomorrow as she found some new cause to embrace.

Running back to my own back porch, I yelled over my shoulder, "Read more Bradbury!"

The future… well, that could thank me later.

The Janus Choice

"Make a hole!"

Danvers heard seconds before being pushed out of the way by a medical tech leading a stretcher team up the ramp to the transition index. He caught a brief glimpse of the body they were carrying and recognized his superior's black-striped tunic. Angry red burns and seeping yellow fluid covered Brandiwicz's face. The arriving team of envoys scattered to either side of the platform to let the medical crew pass. Danvers saw the medics' forms elongate as they entered the index's wavering line and disappear from view.

"You Danvers?" asked a woman as she moved down the ramp, her eyes following the second-wave team as they offloaded additional supplies.

Still in shock, he nodded once. Upon further inspection, he decided she had the look of a traveler—skin worn down by the suns of other worlds, hair bleached and brittle from odd radiations. CERDAIN said the tag on her blue pullover. He wracked his brain, trying to connect the name to any details concerning new arrivals.

"Well, how long will it take you to get me to Brandiwicz?" she asked. "I'm not exactly blessed with a lot of time."

He took a breath and said as evenly as he could manage, "Ma'am, they just took him out on a stretcher. His condition did not look good."

"Huh," she sighed, turning about to look at the transition point. "Well, that turns this whole situation to recycle." Her head snapped back to him. "You're his assistant, right?" She barely gave him a chance to nod in confirmation before continuing, "Well, I hope you're up to it because we need to find out why the Kamanti have suddenly decided we need to leave their world. That transition index will be open for just twenty-four more hours. The next one isn't scheduled until next month."

⌘

"Brandiwicz never had any trouble with the natives before." Danvers shut the gate behind him as he ushered the woman forward. "You're not implying that one of them attacked him, are you?"

"I have no idea. The one person I needed to speak with just went where I can't reach him." She shrugged. "As for a Kamanti harming Brandiwicz, our behavioral model has issues," Cerdain added, swinging up into the passenger seat of the skim. She leaned forward, eyeing the spider-webbing cracks in the windscreen.

"We wouldn't be on the verge of packing up our entire setup and leaving if he were here to give us some idea of what happened. This just keeps getting worse."

Taking a moment to choke back the less-than-respectful replies that came to mind, Danvers managed to say, "It's easy to look at this in a certain way when you are part of the second wave. We've achieved something here with the Kamanti that is the envy of other first-contact teams. Now, with no warning, everything we've put together is going to just vanish. We were notified right before your arrival. As Brandiwicz's assistant, I'll do everything I can to figure out how he was injured and if it is related to this situation." He threw the skim into gear without so much as a glance at her.

Danvers felt her glaring at him and ignored it, pushing the skim out of the rear exit of the embassy compound onto the flat plains and their dark red grasses. Pollen clouds and the winking jewels of the enigmatic light sail farms filled the greenish sky.

Humanity struggled to understand the science behind the machines, making the light sails a prime source of interest to the contact team's scientists. They distributed the power they generated across the planet by wormhole threads. Since it took a massive amount of power to generate transition indexes, the only kind of wormholes humanity knew how to make, there was a definite focus on understanding how the energy transferred from the solar farms to the city below using only a minute amount to initiate the threads.

With a wide arc, Danvers brought them around the exterior of the Diplomatic Compound to the edge of the urban sprawl that surrounded the Kamanti city of Tuanach. Maybe it said something about humanity that they were placed beyond the outskirts of the city and, for the most part, forgotten. Danvers liked to assume it was an honor. He put the errant thought out his head and guided the skim into Tuanach. The city's wide streets gave him plenty of room to maneuver, and he focused on his driving instead of his passenger's ire.

The outpost's director, Weavir, continued to try to find a way back into the good graces of the loose association of Kamanti leaders. Danvers wished him luck. For eight weeks, Danvers enjoyed the pleasures of this world and its unusual people. It looked as though that time could come to an abrupt end. Center punched the transition index through and gave the envoys three months to determine if it was worth the energy cost of making it a permanent settlement.

Since Cerdain's arrival, she acted as if she were going to single-handedly clean up the situation. "Where are we going, Danvers?" she asked, her annoyance clear. "The information I need is back in the compound. Now is not the time for a tour of the city."

"You will want to see where Brandiwicz worked. There could be something in his quarters that will offer more insight into the situation."

"Look, Danvers, why don't you make things clear for me? I talked to Weavir before I got here. I talked to everyone. I even talked to that damned archaeologist, Pergman, who did nothing but complain about the natives' taboo against digging up the past and how he can't do his job. I still can't get a clear answer. Why are we being asked to leave?"

Since they were almost at the set of rooms Brandiwicz was given by the Kamanti, Danvers considered his reply and drove on in silence. After he'd pulled the skim to one side of a low building, he turned to her. "The most difficult part of the situation, ma'am, is that we're not being told to leave. Instead, we were told we can't stay. It is an odd conundrum. Weavir says that he gets the feeling that the Kamanti are acting as if they don't want us involved in something. It's frustrating everyone who's working here. And Pergman, he's just annoying and has a problem with authority."

Cerdain slid out of the skim, her footfalls kicking up the city's ever-present yellow dust. She stood for a moment looking at him across the hood, her arms crossed over her chest. "I know plenty about disappointment, Danvers. Being relegated to clean up someone else's mess is never going to sit well with me."

Danvers turned away as quickly as possible, trying to wipe the scowl off his face. *Who the hell was she, charging in here as if she had any idea what was going on?* He wanted to turn back and argue with Cerdain, but instead, he clenched his hands into fists and led her down a small walk between the rounded walls of the low buildings. He could almost feel the frustration radiating off her. It made him quicken his pace.

The exterior of the building was worn down smooth, like everything in Tuanach. Time lay heavily on the Kamanti. The owner of the sprawling building that housed Brandiwicz's rooms waited for them at the elliptical gate. Danvers was always struck by the fact that the Kamanti were symmetrical in body plan but radially rather than bilaterally.

Their bodies consisted of eight appendages grouped into four legs that led up to a cylindrical waist. The Kamanti arms were arrayed in a square around a central gullet. Like everyone, Danvers got past the desire to look for eyes and stopped trying to categorize them into genders since they reproduced through budding. The skin of the Kamanti not only acted as a receptor of light but also generated it. Like the environs, their skins at rest were dusky yellow broken up by stripes of dark red.

Light rippled across the Kamanti as it walked toward them, photophores in its flesh firing in sequence. Danvers tipped his tablet fleck at the Kamanti, and it began translating.

"For now, you are welcome, associate of Brandiwicz."

Cerdain stepped forward, then Danvers slid sideways to cut her off. Holding the small tablet in front of him, he said with respect to the Kamanti, "Last Light of Day, we are happy to find you here. We must look at Brandiwicz's rooms. Will you let us in?"

It watched the play of colors across the surface of Danvers's computing fleck and replied in kind. "Perhaps you can start to put Brandiwicz's effects in order?"

As Danvers suspected, Cerdain didn't let that pass without a response. Her fleck flashed back at the native, "Is that a request or a demand?"

Turning on its hinged legs, the Kamanti fired back a single flash of light. Danvers turned away, hiding a grin. He suspected that "Yes" was not the answer that Cerdain expected. He leaned over, tugging at the latch on the front door to slide it open, and asked, "Coming, ma'am?"

She impatiently gestured him onward.

Moving inside reminded Danvers of the tremendous flexibility of the Kamanti since the turns from room to room were sinuous without angles. That flexibility was echoed in the spirals inscribed in the walls, typical of Kamanti artwork. As he led Cerdain further into the dwelling, they passed a small kitchen, a cot under a rounded window, and an open garden. At last, they came to a larger area where a contoured desk sat against the curved wall. Cerdain began to shuffle through the items on the top of the desk.

Stepping into the final room, Danvers took a moment to splash water from a low basin onto his face and run his fingers through his close-cropped reddish hair. He looked up at the dingy flex mirror Brandiwicz had tacked to the wall and held back a sigh. His reflection showed tired resignation. He frowned and stepped closer as he noticed something written on the surface of the mirror. Danvers could just make out the words, "Being here doesn't mean you belong." A rather depressing thought backed up by the reality of the current situation. Respect for Brandiwicz outweighed Danvers's guilt as he reached up and wiped away the comment. Cerdain called him when he turned back toward the office.

"What do you make of this, Danvers?"

She considered her fleck with a curious expression. Danvers glanced over her shoulder. The image on the fleck wavered for a moment before a Kamanti came into focus. The viewpoint pulled back until the native could easily be seen. The mirrored surface of one of the many water retention ponds reflected the Kamanti's image. It stood, rocking back and forth, focused on the view before it. Brandiwicz's voice broke into the recording.

"The Kamanti are susceptible to these fits of internal retrospection. It is almost as if they have a problem with being themselves. This, along with other evidence, such as the ingrained aversion to examine their collective past, illustrates how far we are from understanding our hosts."

"So, he knew he was failing? Why wouldn't he ask for help?" Cerdain asked, flipping the fleck back and forth.

"I wouldn't say he was failing. I think that everyone assumed that the Kamanti would be easy to understand since a great deal of their life and culture appears simplistic. But they are alien and radically different from us in many ways. Take, for example, how the Kamanti learn. The Kamanti have something like our mirror neurons. The first time you watch someone do a task, a series of neurons will fire, even though you are not the one doing the task. When you later accomplish the task yourself, this same arc of neurons will fire again.

"The Kamanti have them in droves. We think they educate their young while they are still sessile by imprinting them with layers of visual information that gets absorbed and then acted upon using these mirror neurons. That's like programming their young. It's only once the young become motile that they begin to actively use the information to make choices. This alone makes their culture and their reactions very different from those of humanity."

"If that's the case, then Brandiwicz would have figured that into the overall cultural image of the Kamanti. So, what did he miss?" Not waiting for his answer, Cerdain continued to flip through the fleck chits layered on the top of Brandiwicz's desk. "What do you think, Danvers? Did Brandiwicz do this to himself? The report I read on the way over here said he never regained consciousness before they shipped him out. What can you tell me about his state of mind before his injury?"

"I think sometimes he got frustrated by situations beyond his control. He would have what looked like the answer, and it would turn out to be an inexplicable aspect of the Kamanti behavior never fully observed."

"Yet, you still defend his competency." She sat the fleck down on the desktop for a moment to look at him.

"Up until a day ago, we were very successful here. That success came from the groundwork that Brandiwicz laid. Just because the man had an accident doesn't mean that he is responsible if the mission fails."

Cerdain's fleck chimed. With a faraway look, she considered the message, but the moment did not last. "Gather up all the loose chits. We've got another problem to consider."

He slid his arm across the table, scooping up the remaining info chits before dropping them into his thigh pocket. Then Danvers waved her toward the door. After passing by, Cerdain told him over her shoulder, "Brandiwicz has died. If he didn't injure himself, we're looking at a murder."

Coming to a halt in the doorway, Danvers slumped against the rounded frame. His eyes wouldn't focus, and the dusty yellow of Tuanach faded to a blur. His mentor, colleague, and friend was dead. And the last person he wanted to hear that from walked away. Briefly tempted to slip out the back into Tuanach's winding alleys where Cerdain would never find him, he hesitated. But the chance that she might find out why Brandiwicz perished made him straighten up, pull his tunic straight, and lope after her.

She continued, "If that wasn't bad enough, Pergman has also gone missing. He sent his empty skim back on autopilot. Your staff is annoyed. We're asked to retrieve him since we're closest."

Danvers opened his mouth to tell her about Pergman's personal tracking tag, but Cerdain cut him off, "And just in case you weren't certain, that annoys *me*." She headed toward the entrance, not waiting for Danvers to show her out.

At the doorway, Danvers stopped and looked back. Still in shock over Brandiwicz's death, something unexpected caught his attention. By the entrance was a little alcove. Usually empty, it now held something. Stepping closer, he reached in to pull out a strange, brown object, about the size of his thumb, hollow and covered in unusual rectangular markings, sealed at one end. The other terminus ended in a jagged edge. The design on the outside caught his attention. Kamanti artwork was full of spirals, not squares. What was he looking at? Perplexed, Danvers took it with him.

Cerdain was already in the driver's seat, tapping her fingers on the dash. "Get in. I never planned on collecting missing team members. Who knows what the hell happened to Pergman..."

Danvers leaned back as the skim shot forward. "He's not in danger. The Kamanti are not a violent species."

"Not violent? Look, just because they are not actively seeking to hurt you doesn't mean that they won't step out of the way and let you take the hit."

"Ma'am, I can't say that I agree with most of your views." He paused to look down at his fleck, then pointed to the right. "Wait, take a right here." He looked at his fleck again. "According to the locator on Pergman, he's way out in the foothills past the edge of the plains."

The skim picked up speed, its air-cushion protecting them from the uneven portions of the terrain. Looking over at Cerdain as she pushed the skim faster and faster, Danvers broached the question that gnawed at him. "Ma'am, is there a particular reason you happen to be unhappy with Pergman and Brandiwicz?"

She gave him a sharp glance and drove on, remaining silent. The awkward moment continued.

"If you must know, Danvers... we are having a great deal of trouble with the cultural modeling program we are running. I can only assume that our two most direct information sources must be flawed, hence my displeasure. We cannot nail down the correct behavior model for the Kamanti." She took a breath. "Therefore, we can't come up with their reasons behind this sudden about-face. With the data we've received so far, I only have a month to get this running properly. I don't consider failure an option. Our part of this expedition was to be next. Since receiving word of the Kamanti's desire for us to vacate, Center has given the whole embassy two days to finish its mission. At that point, the transition index will open, and Weavir needs to be ready to give them a yea or nay."

"So, I take it that the cultural modeling is your project?"

"If you must ask, it's unlikely you'll ever be called perceptive." Cerdain shook her head and turned her attention back to driving, shutting him out completely.

Watching the buildings diminish as the skim lifted out onto the plain, Danvers looked back at Tuanach. *There is still so much to learn from the Kamanti,* he mused. Their natural command over light gives them a unique perspective on such subjects as luminous data storage and light propulsion. Never mind that the natives were close-mouthed about their biology and even more reticent to talk about their past. With its casual mix of technology and massive communal living, this amazing world remained a rich treasure trove of knowledge.

A mile-long plume of yellow dust trailed after the skim as the heat from the plains rose in shimmering waves. Danvers spared a glance at Cerdain. Wisps of lighter hair fanned out around her head and danced about in the wind. Her blue-and-red-striped embassy pullover bunched and rucked at her hips. Her clenched grasp on the steering column made the tendons in her hands stand up like cords. Focused on the goal, she could miss things like potential solutions.

Glancing at her fleck, Cerdain adjusted their course away from the light farms overhead and said, "I don't have to worry about driving us through one of the wormhole threads transmitting power, do I?"

"There's no physical connection between the light sail farm and the receivers in the city. It's just not possible." Danvers realized his tone was a bit sharp and added, "So much of the Kamanti technology is passive in nature. The truth is, I'm jealous of them. It doesn't break down, so they don't worry about it. As a civilization, they've reached a point where infrastructure is no longer an issue." For a moment, he considered her. An odd question, surely, she knew — then he had it. She probed at him, probably wondering how much he knew about the wormhole threads.

The tension drained out of Cerdain. "Don't get me wrong, Danvers. I want this to work. It *has* to work. Don't ever think that I'm not impressed by what I've seen in my short time here. But keep in mind that I am building a cultural model that will give future expeditions an immediate head-start to understanding the Kamanti. Which, if things do not change, will be useless."

Danvers looked away. Her abrasive nature was back again. *A very short moment of calm in a perpetual storm*, he thought.

The skim approached the hills now as they headed into canyon country. Soon, Cerdain banked back and forth as they entered the maze of arroyos. She forced the skim higher on its air-cushion as Danvers checked his fleck. They were about two kilometers from Pergman.

"Down there," Cerdain motioned, turning the skim 180 degrees to plunge into a tight gully. Light filtered down along the reddish walls of stone, giving everything a ruddy cast. The skim came to an abrupt halt, throwing Danvers toward the windscreen. Pushing himself back, he resisted the urge to snap.

The arroyo narrowed to a winding path, and Cerdain brought them to a halt in the last possible flat space. Fleck held in front of her, she slid out and headed to the left. Light from the display's surface playing over her features had Danvers imagining what she might look like in conversation with the Kamanti, and he almost smiled. He climbed out, silently berated himself, and found his footing on the rough ground, ready to follow her between the looming walls of the canyon. Colored bands crawled through the twisting columns of rock formed by the very wind-borne sands that annoyed his eyes now.

"Only a damn archaeologist would enjoy coming here," Cerdain called over her shoulder.

"Or a geologist."

"Don't feel you need to argue with me on principal, Danvers."

Another smile crossed his lips. Turning one final corner, they found their way blocked by a mound of scree and rubble. "Well, that's new," Danvers remarked as he dropped to one knee to gather up a handful of the ocher dirt, sifting it through his fingers.

"Looks like your archaeologist ignored restrictions."

"Pergman. Well, he was never very good at following orders to the letter."

"Now you're wondering if this is the reason behind our sudden need to leave the planet," Cerdain said dryly, "You're not the only one. Any wonder why Weavir felt it necessary to hit him with a tracking tag... ?" She'd reached the top of the rockfall and stopped with her hands on her hips. "Get up here. You won't believe this."

As Danvers pulled himself up, he realized they were on the edge of a large, bowl-shaped excavation. But that was the rim. At its center, a tunnel descended out of sight. "Weavir's going to have Pergman's head."

"He can get in line. I'm here first," Cerdain replied, waspishly. Already she'd stalked over to the guide rope running from the rim to the tunnel and began to make her way down.

Danvers followed. He had little choice. A string of tiny, blue-white lights descended into the depths along the ceiling of the tunnel. Together they went downward.

Their descent was rapid once he got used to Cerdain randomly tugging on the line below him. Danvers stopped, looking closely at the patterning on the wall of the tunnel. He'd missed something. There were spiraling grooves the whole way down. Almost as if— "Bastard," he snapped, slapping the wall.

"Figured it out?" Cerdain asked, moving onward, "Pergman ought to hope I just seal up this tunnel and forget about it. Unlicensed and unapproved use of nano-dissociators. Whatever career he had, it's over. I hope the natives don't exercise any of their territorial rights."

Increasing the speed of his descent, Danvers slid along the scree, trying to catch up. In fact, he moved so quickly that when the tunnel's pitch leveled out, he fell forward. Cerdain reached down and caught his hand, hauling him to his feet. Struck by her silence and the intensity of her stare, following her gaze, he saw the first of the immense cylinders.

They were a dark, coppery red. The glow from brighter lights stuck to the ceiling fell onto three of the objects. Danvers walked up the closest and reached out a hand. He caught himself before touching the cylinder, mesmerized by its strange, indistinct nature. Call it a hunch, but something about the patina made him pull out his fleck and do a quick scan. Viewed with higher magnification, it became obvious an immense number of tiny hook-like cilia covered the exterior of the cylinder, all of which were canted upward. Upon further inspection, Danvers saw that the cilia moved in a spiral pattern almost too slowly to be seen.

"Don't... " he warned and then stopped, realizing that Cerdain now looked over his shoulder at the fleck's image instead of reaching out as he had.

"Can't imagine what touching that would do, but I'm not going to give it a try. Consider this for a second. If you were to bury that cylinder in the ground, wouldn't the cilia propel it back up to the surface?"

Stepping around the circumference, Danvers looked down at yet another hole. Pergman had been quite busy. He wondered how far below the cylinders' origins lay. And the real reason behind all of this? Something else caught his eye. Rectangular shapes were embossed on the cylinder's exterior. One had to account for the cylinder's size and the bad lighting, but the shapes were familiar. He pulled out the small cylinder he found in Brandiwicz's rooms. He started to call out to Cerdain but noticed a shadow moving across the light at the far end of the tunnel.

Cerdain moved forward. "Pergman! What the hell is going on here?"

Circling around the cylinder, Danvers put on a burst of speed, trying to intercept her before the encounter turned violent.

The archaeologist stopped mid-stride, a stunned look on his face. His long hair pulled back in clumps of dreadlocks, and the single suit he wore streaked with multicolored dust. A series of programmable plastic tables were arranged in an arc behind him. Various implements lay scattered about on top of specimen bins. In the middle lay a very familiar rod-like shape that mirrored the one in Danvers's pocket.

"Did Weavir send you? I'm not quite ready yet. There's so much more to find here. We've got to take the time and pack things up properly."

"Properly?" Tension and anger marred Cerdain's features as she marched forward, hands clenched at her sides. "Tell me why the unauthorized use of nano-dissociators, excavation against the express permission of the natives, and the use of embassy property to accomplish your personal agenda would have anything in common with doing this in a proper fashion?"

"Wait," Danvers interrupted, "you're saying that Weavir is aware of what you're doing here?"

"Certainly," Pergman said, indignation wrinkling up his features, "and I also gave all of my findings to Brandiwicz."

Sharing a brief look with Cerdain, Danvers took a breath before continuing. "Well, I think maybe our anger may be a bit misdirected. Pergman, just what is going on here?"

Pergman took several steps back and pulled a sling chair out from behind the worktables. He slid back into it and proceeded to stare at the two intruders. Leaning forward, he spread his hands and said, "What we don't know about this culture is staggering. Even now, I've made some finds that I can barely explain. There are elements at work here that run beneath the veneer of Kamanti society. But before I could really start digging into things, Brandiwicz stepped in. Weavir will hold him responsible."

"Brandiwicz is dead," Cerdain snapped, "So that's hardly relevant."

Pergman sat stunned for a moment, his mouth open. But quick with the rejoinder, he asked, "Who the hell are you?"

"This is Cerdain, she is with the second-wave team and in charge of the Kamanti behavioral model," Danvers said. Then he asked, "Just what did you find?"

"I found the one thing hidden right in front of us all along, evidence of a second race... the Mahanti.

"When I look at the Kamanti, I see a culture that has worn down so many of its distinguishing marks that it reminds me of a river pebble. You can keep trying to get a grasp on it, but it slips away every time. There are plenty of aspects of the Kamanti that just don't add up. But they are so old, as a species, that they've tinkered with their biology and psychology. But the basics of their makeup, now that's where things get interesting."

"Academics." Cerdain shook her head in disgust. "Can you get to the point?"

Danvers intervened. "Start with something simple. What are the cylinders?"

Pergman took a deep breath. He started to answer but stopped, unsure of what to reveal. Steepling his hands in front of his face, he said quietly, "Those are the arks that hold the Mahanti culture. At least this set is. The deep resonance wave scans show another set even further down. After that, there's another and another. It's like there are waves of them launched from some set of machines deep down in the mantle. They are all over this world, slowly digging their way up. I had to dig down fifteen miles just to get these." The archaeologist got to his feet, walking over to stand in front of the closest cylinder. "This," he said, motioning toward the towering object, "just screams time capsule to me. Look, the Kamanti didn't want us prying into their history because they are culturally programmed not to. They didn't want us investigating their biology because it might reveal things about their nature."

Pergman stopped and looked at Cerdain, studying her face. The mask of indifference she'd put on slipped for a moment.

Pointing a finger at her, he said, "You knew. You knew about their biology. I wonder where that information came from."

She looked down, unwilling to meet either of their gazes. "I needed to, in order to properly flesh out the cultural model."

"So, just where did you get this information from?" Danvers demanded, feeling his own ire rising. All the double-dealing and maneuvering finally pushed him to the breaking point.

"Gathered surreptitiously, of course. Samples taken here and there. Discrete probes sent out," Cerdain replied.

"More nanotech, right?" Danvers asked with a touch of anger.

"Of course. But you see, Danvers, what we discovered didn't answer any of our questions. We found out that the Kamanti rebuilt their biology."

"Okay, so that's something new to me, but what does it have to do with the Mahanti? What were they?"

Cerdain looked to Pergman for the answer. He walked behind a cylinder tapping his lip. When he reappeared, he said, "The Mahanti and Kamanti were co-extant species, both of which could have developed into the natural owners of this world. Their biology was very similar: both radially symmetric, photophore bearing, and exceptional in terms of intelligence. If you look at the basements of the buildings of Tuanach, you'll find there are foundations upon foundations upon foundations. The city is built up like a nautilus shell. Go down far enough, and there's a point where the architecture changes to something more angular in nature. At that point, you're looking at the Mahanti's work." The archaeologist's hand hovered over the cylinder in admiration. "When I looked at resonance photos of deeply buried cities, I found spiraling architecture down so far, and then the rest was all angular. Go on down, and you find more spirals once again. At some point, the cultures realized that one of them would become dominant and supersede the other. Humanity didn't share Earth with the Neanderthals, and these two cultures realized they couldn't either."

"So, the Kamanti were the winners, and now they have collective cultural guilt because of it. Then we come along and discover the truth by breaking a taboo that requires us to leave. Have I got it?" Cerdain summarized.

Danvers stepped closer to the specimen tables as an argument commenced. He reached down and picked up a small, hollow cylinder. It matched the one from his pocket. The same angular designs covered its exterior. Interestingly enough, they were laid out in a spiral pattern. Here it was, the two aspects of the civilizations mated together. An idea began to form. Pieces slid together in his mind, shaping the larger framework of the puzzle.

Danvers cleared his throat. Pergman and Cerdain both paused to look at him. Holding up the two halves of the cylindrical container, Danvers asked, "Just what was in this?"

Pergman looked at it for a second and then answered, "A dull, translucent rod decorated with more of the same inscription. One of these is at the center of every one of the time capsules."

"Can I guess that you gave the rod to Brandiwicz?"

"Yes, he asked for it specifically when I showed him the inventory. Wait, what are you implying?"

"Not yet, please," Danvers said and then turned to Cerdain. "If you had to guess, just how extensively have the Kamanti modified themselves?"

"Quite a bit. It's almost as if they decided to refine their life processes and do away with any evolutionary dead ends. Since I've just heard about the Mahanti, I can't make any comparisons. So, if you're asking, did they try to blend the species, I can't say."

"It's not that that simple," Danvers answered. "I think we made a lot of assumptions when we tried to find out what happened here. We looked at things on our timescale. We look at how humans would make any given decision, clouding our findings." He looked at the cylinder again. "Maybe you were right, Pergman, but it's not a time capsule... more like a recipe." Danvers took a breath and then asked, "How long would it take one of these cylinders to reach the surface?"

Pergman scratched at his chin. "I don't know. A quarter of a million years? Longer? You're saying that they were seeded at that depth so they would reappear on the surface at some point in the future?"

"I think that makes sense," Cerdain replied, "But look, we have more information now. We should get that to Weavir. There is even the possibility that we can use what we know to convince the Kamanti to let us stay."

Danvers looked about the confined area. There didn't seem to be a reason to stay anymore. "I vote to leave."

"Fine," Pergman replied and then took a brief tour around the area, shutting down anything still running. He reached into a carry sack and pulled out a small winch motor. "This will make it easier for us to get out."

"For you maybe, but what about us?" Cerdain asked.

"Oh, I'll just lower it down the hole again."

"In that case, I'll go first," she said, grabbing the small motor from the archaeologist. Within seconds she'd vanished from sight. The winch slid down the cable after a little while, and Pergman ascended next.

Slightly surprised, Danvers reached for the machine when it arrived for him. Both Cerdain and Pergman had something to hide. He hesitated, looking around. Even though he'd suggested leaving, there were still a great many unanswered questions here. Then he worked his way up the tunnel.

Brandiwicz would have understood. The message on his mirror said it all. The divide between the thought processes of the Kamanti/Mahanti and humanity couldn't be breached. It could only be approximated. The solution that the two races created was simply too alien.

Danvers reached up and grasped Pergman's offered hand when he reached the edge of the excavation. Swinging back, he looked down. A hole almost as full of secrets as the people he worked with brought him up short. The kind of secrets one would kill for? Cerdain and Pergman stared at him as he turned away from the dig site. He climbed into the back seat, Cerdain took the driver's seat, and the archeologist slid in beside her. It was a long, quiet ride back to the compound.

When they reached the edge of Tuanach, Danvers recognized a very familiar figure just off the edge of the road to the Diplomatic Compound. He tapped Cerdain on the shoulder. "I'll walk from here." She looked at him sharply but brought the skim to a halt. As they drove away, Danvers saw their heads lean together; just how many of the details of their conspiracy would be hatched after he left? He turned back to the Kamanti edging forward out of the shadows.

He looked at the patterns on the Kamanti's skin. What was Last Light of Day doing here? Before he could bring his fleck up to ask the question, the Kamanti lit up with a rush of color.

"Why are you here?" it asked.

Danvers hesitated. Every time he spoke to a Kamanti, it felt like there existed an extra level of depth to their conversation that he didn't quite grasp. Even now, he wasn't certain that the question was meant for him or humanity as a whole. Perhaps it was best to limit the potential for error. "The others left me behind." Realizing he might not get the opportunity again, he transmitted to the fleck a question, "Last Light of Day, did Brandiwicz ever show you something, something important?"

The native didn't answer him. Instead, it shuffled around him and took a few steps down the roadway back toward Tuanach. When it turned back, Last Light of Day leaned toward Danvers, a human affectation that Brandiwicz taught them, to indicate to whom they were speaking. His fleck translated, "He showed me the future and the past all in one flash."

Danvers approached the Kamanti. "He showed you a rod, and that rod flashed you with a burst of information."

"No," Last Light of Day replied, "I saw the light of other ideas. Ideas I can't forget, ideas that are not part of what it means to be Kamanti." The Kamanti's light swirled. "Danvers, I glow with these ideas. Others look at me, and they see the ideas, and then they are part of them as well. I went into the crèche as I always do. I shared with the young. But I couldn't share the things they needed to know. No, I shared with them this infestation that is changing me. I look at myself, and I am not me! Danvers, what did he do to us?"

Stepping back, Danvers covered his eyes. It must have seemed like the perfect solution at the time. Bury the capsules but allow them to return after ages of the Kamanti civilization so it could be the Mahanti's turn. Beyond them further still was another fleet of capsules digging their way up to recreate the Kamanti once more. How long had the cycle gone on? Yet, no one counted on some external force with more curiosity than common sense. Did Brandiwicz ever realize what he'd done?

Could one write memes in luminous information? The Kamanti would take it in with no buffers since they were taught that way during childhood. Add a compulsion to share, and a self-propagating reiteration of an entire culture occurred in cycles.

The Kamanti were right. Humanity did not belong here. Humanity started the process prematurely in ignorance. That same ignorance could infect the nascent society forming and corrupt everything, every being.

Dropping his hands, he forced his eyes open. With the fleck, he spoke heavy with regret, "I would like to believe Brandiwicz made a mistake. He did show you your future, a future decided upon by your distant ancestors. One not meant to happen for many more years. I think he made a mistake, intending no harm." He paused, trying to come up with more, wondering if Brandiwicz did this intentionally trying to discover the technology behind the wormhole threads hidden in the cultural download. The Kamanti, however, wanted to have the last word.

"You do not have to go, but you cannot stay. Tuanach is not safe for you." With that enigmatic comment, it turned and walked slowly into the city.

Danvers watched the small form grow indistinct. As he turned back, he faced the Diplomatic Compound's high wall and began his own walk. When he neared the gate, Danvers became aware of movement overhead. Typically, they were so high up he ignored them, but the light sail farms were clustering together, their indistinct white forms moving into an eye-blearing sheet. Danvers could not say what survival instinct made him run, but he threw himself through the gate. Turning quickly, he shut the heavy door and rolled into the shadow of the curving wall.

An incandescent flash bounced from every surface of the Compound above him. A profound silence followed, finally broken by a loud hiss, like a rising wind. When the pressure wave struck, the Compound rang like a giant bell, and the omnipresent yellow dust flew over everything like a cyclone.

When they found him, Danvers huddled against the wall. The others from the Diplomatic team pulled him to his feet and slung his arms over their shoulders. Together they stumbled into the Compound. When they reached the second floor, Danvers caught a glimpse of the sheet of molten magma that once was Tuanach. The light sail farms passed several of the mouths of the wormhole threads over the city, reducing it to a glowing ember. Just like everything else the Kamanti and Mahanti built, even the premature launch of a civilization had a fail-safe built into it. That defined their technology to a point—it just worked.

Eventually, Cerdain collected every one of the chits from Danvers. He handed them over without resistance. Maybe one of them contained the secret they were seeking, the creation and control of wormhole threads. He hoped not. After all, they'd just survived a demonstration of how powerful a weapon they could be. She left him the small hollowed-out end of the container for the rod that started everything.

Looking down at the city's cooling remains, Danvers reconsidered the logic behind the Compound's placement. Maybe the Kamanti tried to protect themselves from the humans, but the buildings were just far enough away to survive the kind of strike that destroyed Tuanach. The etchings on the cylinder dug into his palm as Danvers clutched it tight. He tried to crush it, remove all reminders of Last Light of Day and Brandiwicz's fate. But it was stronger than he thought. Looking down, Danvers realized perhaps he needed something to remind himself that he didn't have all the answers. Finally, he turned his back on the sea of charred lava below, certain that even such a huge memorial to hubris would have very little effect on humanity in the long run.

No Visitors Beyond This Point

WHEN THE SMALL SHIPS CAME OUT OF TRANSITION ABOVE THE ravaged world, their flocking behavior briefly confused the defense system. X-ray lasers fired into the path of the avoy scouting mission from the debris field before them. One by one, the fleet's brassy chevrons were brought down to spiral through the toxic atmosphere and crash onto the ruins of the world below.

"Kendell, you know who got you elected."

Kendell rolled over as Bran's voice came again, "Wake up!"

In the resulting pause, Representative Kendell had the house system pass the incoming transmission to his implant. He glared owlishly as the image of Bran hovered in the corner of his vision. "Fine, Bran, you've got my undivided attention. You wanted to talk to me, so talk."

"Well, it's a good thing you're already reclining. You'd want to take this one sitting down. An archaic defense net shot down an avoy scout swarm on a backwater piece of rock just inside our territory."

Kendell exhaled raggedly, and his shoulders slumped.

Bran stepped into the conversational gap. "Here's what we know. Fourteen hours ago, your time, seventeen avoy scouts dropped into the orbital plane of an Obsidian-listed planet. X-ray lasers from a legacy system located on the lunar remnants systematically shot them down. A tachyon pulse was sent out before all the ships were destroyed, so the news is already out there. An inquest is in the process of being prepared according to our sources." Bran sighed and then continued, "You must realize how delicate this situation is."

Kendell rolled over and planted his feet on the floor. Obsidian-listed. Only one Obsidian-listed world really mattered, and no one below his pay grade knew about it. "So, the galactics are already moving on this? What can we do?"

"Actually, it's not as bad as it seems."

The representative gave Bran's image a stare as if questioning his sanity. "How the hell do you see it as less than catastrophic? Seventeen lives lost when our standing is already fragile with the galactics."

"The avoy were admittedly far off-course, inside the fringe of our claimed territory. An unmanned system attacked them. A legacy structure, a remnant of our past exploration. This is a regrettable accident, nothing more."

Pulling on an insulsuit, Kendell stopped, one arm into the sleeve. "You know damn well that this could become a very regrettable incident for us, one that might drastically affect our standing in the Galactic Community."

"Right now, I have a very carefully picked group recovering the wreckage. They will also 'ensure' that the defense system is no longer operational. We need to do some damage control here and shift the focus from this being our fault. If we can get this cleaned up before anyone from the inquest group arrives, perhaps we can pass off the necessity of their visiting the area," Bran offered, leaning back in his chair.

"Despite what you're saying, I think we need to tread lightly here. There's still anti-alien sentiment present in the populace. Secrets can come back and bite us, Bran. I'll just have to do my best to resolve the issue," Kendall said with a sigh as he stepped from his quarters.

"You're a representative of Governance; the thousands of species in the Diversiform want to believe you. Governance is the voice they believe because they must. It's the same all over. It doesn't matter if it's a shiapt ambassador withholding the truth about their bloody ritual scarring or that the wickurn never really mentioning that they change sex after they go through a bloom, or better yet that we are talking to ten different yenbeyor all pretending to be the same ambassador because we can't tell them apart. Every species has its secrets."

Walking into one of the concourses, Kendell stopped to look up through the overhead dome. The halo of inhabited asteroids arced over the station. Spidery webs of elevators and transport links glistened like reflective wire. "But *those* galactics didn't just shoot down seventeen unarmed scouts."

Bran thought for a moment and then replied, "There are species that refuse to supply their back history. You can't tell me that there isn't a good reason for that. There could be atrocities that would shock anyone among the histories of the Community."

Kendell looked directly at the image, staring down Bran, "But this is us. Our standing is still fragile. It still stirs up the public that we gave up nineteen worlds that we were in the process of terraforming to the Community for their Diversiform Dispute. The whole idea of competing for worlds by creating the best biospheres for them is something humanity is only beginning to understand. We're a very young species in an old galaxy full of inhabitants who use an established system to determine who has the right to develop discovered worlds. Even after the Diaspora gave us so many worlds, sometimes it still feels like we're spread too thin. If the galactics sanction us, things could explode."

"Kendell, you're treating this as if we have a choice. We don't. Given your location on Novya, you are the closest representative. You need to be prepared. Wait, there's more news. Word just came down that the inquest is accepting our recovery of the wreckage. The avoy are actually apologizing for the incursion into what could be conceived as our space. But there's a catch, the inquest is sending an observer, an imesht."

"Damn."

"Tomorrow at ten local; the observer will expect a meeting. Kendell, I won't waste my breath telling you how important it is that this is handled well."

"Thanks for the spotlight, Bran. I'll get an area set aside to receive the wreckage."

"Keep in touch, Kendell, and don't forget, I made sure you got this post for just such emergencies."

Hoping his brisk pace would move the stimulant he'd just drank through his system, Kendell walked through the hangar bay, serving as a temporary mortuary and investigation area. Mentally, he had prepared himself for a number of things except for the smell, a strange mixture of pepper and rust. An hour before his scheduled meeting with the imesht, things were pretty well wrapped up.

The avoy corpses were a surprise. Kendell expected them to make the white polyon body bags look like tents due to their 'V' shaped flight surfaces, which were perpetually canted at an angle. But in most cases, the bags resided in tubs, which bespoke horrific damage to the bodies. The plunge through the atmosphere and subsequent impact made it difficult to separate the pilot from the ship. Since three ships' integrity failed, their wreckage ended up scattering over an area too wide to easily recover. The closer he looked, the more nauseous he became. Fourteen recovered bodies from an incident that should have never occurred. That thought would certainly not occur to Bran. The helanx, Tunegura, one of the investigative technicians, recognizing him, rolled over. Kendell took a brief look around, assuring himself there was nothing else to be seen. "Let's go outside. You can give me the details there."

Kendell walked alongside the alien until they reached one of the lounge areas. He led the helanx over to the fountain that took up a corner of the room, knowing that Tunegura would appreciate the water. Splashing briefly in the shallow end of the pool, the helanx spun on its axis to point one side of its circular body toward Kendell. Kendell briefly considered pulling over a seat for the alien but realized it was happier in the pool. The water the helanx ingested and pumped through the hard round surface allowed the body to use magnetic fields to spin the wheel, providing motion. An improvement over the old days where Tunegura would have pushed himself along with the three thin arms that grew around the rim on each side. Thin fingers and keen eyesight made Tunegura an excellent technician and mechanic.

"What did you find?" Kendell asked, leaning against the backrest.

The center eye on this side of Tunegura bobbled briefly on its stalk and then came back to point at him. From the voice box slung under the eyestalk came the words, "The equipment survived the impact fairly well. The pilots did not. Too much force applied too quickly to delicate bodies. The ships, disabled by the laser strikes, unable to compensate, were pulled down by gravity. Avoy flyers are not designed for use in atmosphere."

Kendell steepled his hands in front of his mouth. "Were you able to find out if this was the actual destination or an accident?"

Rolling forward slightly and rocking from side to side, Tunegura replied, "The information in the system is fairly specific. The transition brought the group out within a reasonable margin of error from where they arrived."

Kendell noticed the eye no longer looking directly looked at him. "Was there anything else?"

"It is possible that the coordinates were in a message. The communication equipment recovered suffered considerable damage, but information in a buffer bears a transmission mark. It could be a message containing the coordinates."

"But you can't verify that?"

"No. There... " the helanx hesitated. Spinning backward to the lip of the pool, Tunegura wavered from side to side. Suddenly, Kendell realized there was a presence behind him. Turning slowly and forcing himself not to flinch, he discovered the imesht representative looming over the back of his chair. The scant description of the species left Kendell unprepared for meeting the imesht. Resting on six multi-jointed legs, its long, thin body curved three meters upward into the air. At its upper end were three pairs of what he assumed were arms. Two pairs were folded behind the imesht's back in a very human fashion, and one of the remaining limbs extended toward him. Putting out his hand, Kendall very gently shook the extremity. It felt as smooth as glass on the top and ridged on the bottom. The whole body was no thicker than his thigh and covered in a short, black coat of fur, with two reddish-brown circular areas at either end.

"Please excuse my entrance. I am told we are much quieter than most other species. Some find it disturbing."

Kendell had no idea where the sound emanated from, so it was likely artificial. He shrugged off the distraction.

"Representative, I am glad you were able to come so soon. I just finished getting a preliminary report from the investigative team. Perhaps you have some questions for the technician?" Kendall said, pointing toward the Tunegura

In the intervening moment, the helanx took the opportunity to leave the fountain and rolled around to come to a stop before them both. Before it could say anything, the imesht interrupted.

"I will consider the report when it is complete. That would be the wisest course. After all, we have determined that this is an accident. We are merely performing due diligence here. Thank you, technician. That will be all."

The Tunegura rotated slightly toward Kendell, its eyestalk swiveling in his direction. While tempted to ask the helanx to continue its conversation, Kendall found something in the imesht's tone that made him hesitate. Instead, Kendall nodded to the small alien. Accepting his dismissal, Tunegura rolled back toward the hangar area.

"Perhaps we can adjourn to the ambassadorial suite and continue our discussion more privately," suggested the imesht, tipping backward to rest on the six limbs at its opposite end. Kendell suddenly struggled with the possibility that he didn't know which end was the head. *Did the alien have a head, per se?* The statement convinced Kendell that more went on here than a simple resolution to the incident. As he got to his feet to lead the imesht down the corridor, he sent a request through one of his communications implants asking that Tunegura wait until he was free. Something in that last interrupted statement might clear up the nature of the unease growing in his mind.

The lighting flickering briefly as the alien adjusted the room's settings, Kendell followed the imesht into the ambassadorial suite. The door slid shut behind him, and he flinched as the lights went out. Standing in the dark, with a nearly silent alien, in a room now under imesht sovereignty… *Could it get any worse?* he thought. The familiar vista of Novya came into view as the imesht used the projection units in the suite. The hazy globe hung above them, garlanded in a ring of asteroid satellites and a filmy web of junctions. Kendell could see the alien silhouetted against the Novya shine. With a long limb, it reached up, indicating a star. The projection warped, the starfield bending as the viewpoint rushed closer to this sun with its series of planets—the system where the accident occurred.

Kendell called to mind everything he could remember about the imesht. The aliens were reclusive, never involving themselves in the Community unless it was beneficial to them. They were neighbors to human space. The projection narrowed in on the planet in question. Kendall advanced on the imesht. In the reflected light, its body fur rapidly shifted color through a series of flashing ripples Kendell found difficult to look at. He stood there a moment, fists clenching, as a pristine Moon looped gracefully about a green Earth. An image that no one outside of Governance should ever see. A dark secret come back to haunt him and now in the hands of another. The notations indicated the same Obsidian-listed world, the site of the avoy accident. 350 years ago, the location of Earth was lost, and the general populace believed that story. The story of the disaster that brought about the Diaspora remained more a deliberate legend than history.

"We heard you."

That was all the imesht said for the moment. Pushing the tension out of his body, Kendell dropped his hands to his sides. The alien obviously read human reactions. Telegraphing his did him no favors. "We can be noisy."

Moving around again so that it became once again visible, the imesht continued, "We heard the many broadcasts from your former home. We know where you came from. We've had concerns about your introduction to the Galactic Community."

Behind its tall form, the spinning Earth slowly grew darker as reddish stains appeared in the atmosphere. Flickering lights lit up the cloud cover from below. Bright pinpoints of yellow seared through the red stains. Then the Moon came apart on its next rotation. Calving like a great iceberg into pieces, it rained down on the formerly verdant Earth.

"Even after your bombardment, the eaters that you made blindly ingested your world. You destroyed your homeworld in an act of barbarism. Perhaps that is why you have become so good at creating new homes."

At the heart of the dissolving Moon, other shapes formed. Rugged and angular, the great ships of the Diaspora were born from the bones of the Moon. One of the limbs of the imesht rose, the image changing again, pulling back to the Novya solar system. Ten light-years whipped by in the wave of a limb. The world now rotating in the center of the ambassadorial suite revealed a dull black and gray globe with thin wisps of clouds. As a Diaspora ship fell into orbit about it, the planet lit with impact after impact, water-bearing comets falling downward. Time shifted in the presentation. Years whirring by in seconds. Novya rapidly grew green, and the web of the asteroids spun into existence. The projection ended abruptly, and Kendell found the imesht looming over him once again.

He forced himself not to backpedal away from it. Now he understood the alien's intentions. The imesht wanted humanity's improved terra-forming technology, or else they would reveal the nature of the destruction of Earth to the Galactic Community. In a culture based on the competitive development of ecospheres, such a stain on humanity's past would be a massive loss of face. What could he do about its unspoken demand? As the representative on world, he couldn't implement policy on such broad terms. Perhaps a delaying tactic remained the best answer.

"I will have to speak to Governance concerning this."

The imesht drew back slightly. "You do not claim to represent Governance?"

"Of course, I represent them. But I do not speak for all of Governance. Governance is an agreement of all the representatives of the settled worlds. In matters with wide-ranging effects such as this, it is necessary to gain the consensus of the whole."

The imesht shook itself briefly and stepped to one side daintily. "I represent the entirety of the imesht interests here. There is no reason why you should not be able to do the same."

Kendal now advanced, pointing a finger at the imesht. "You've made an assumption. That does not make it a truth."

Once again, the alien pulled itself up to its full height. "You have twenty hours to make a decision. Otherwise, we will share the information about your past with the rest of the Community. It is regrettable that you cannot make this decision yourself, but we will wait only so long for your consensus."

The imesht turned abruptly and moving to the far side of the room. Kendell stood there for a moment. Apparently, he was dismissed.

Outside of the ambassadorial suite, leaning against the wall, Kendall thought furiously. There were things here that didn't make sense. He queried his data-stores about the imesht once again. Amid reading the information, Kendell came to a stop. He made another query, one he should have before. As he read, Kendell pulled up the report concerning the avoy wreckage. His concern deepened. His pace increasing, Kendell sent out a request for the technician, followed by a request for a ship from the Governance port.

"What can we find here that we did not find out before?" Tunegura asked as reentry buffeted the small shuttle.

Kendell looked over at the helanx strapped into its concave depression. "How many avoy were recovered?"

"Fourteen out of the seventeen ships that were observed."

"And how badly damaged were those ships in consideration of the avoy design and the situation?"

Hesitating a moment, Tunegura answered, "They were in very poor shape. The landing party indicated that the remaining ships were completely destroyed and unrecoverable."

Kendell met the helanx's gaze for a moment and nodded. "Have a look at this information as well. I had a second autopsy performed on the avoy."

He shunted a file across to the alien concerning the physical makeup of the bodies.

All six of the small alien's arms slapped against the surface of its wheel. "This makes no sense. It is not reasonable. You are saying that all the avoy in the scouting party were nymphs? There were no adults in the swarm?"

Kendell turned back to monitor their descent toward the surface of what had once been Earth. "Yes. More importantly, do you recall how avoy regard their young?"

"Avoy consider the nymphs to be unintelligent things until they reach their final molt and assume adulthood. Due to their breeding practices, they will occasionally even sell ... " The helanx trailed off. "The signal, you think that this is all a construction. No, that is not the phrase. You mean a 'set up.'"

"Yes, and I expect that the remaining three ships were probably in better shape and could still be down here. I'm starting a search pattern now. If we can establish the origin of the signal that guided the ships, I may be able to tie this all back to one source."

Tunegura stood silent for a moment. "What made you think in such a convoluted fashion?"

"I remembered your comment about the signal. Someone else made a statement about listening, and I guess the two brought things together."

The helanx turned to the controls mounted on either side of its body, its tiny hands flickering over the surfaces. "Here, this is a more efficient search pattern. Look, already the system has found one of the scout ships."

"I'm sending a probe down," Kendell replied, pointing the shuttle in the direction Tunegura indicated.

The helanx remained silent when the information from the probe reached the shuttle. Kendell waited as long as he dared and then asked slowly, "Well?"

"The pilot is definitely a nymph at the last stage of its development. At this point, they are intelligent enough to fall into the Community's definition of sapience."

"That's not exactly the information I asked about," Kendell said with a sigh.

Tunegura fell silent once more, although Kendell could see the information filling its control screens.

"Tunegura, please..."

"Perhaps it is not as important as you believe."

"What?"

"Kendell, you should look at this."

Their ship was destroyed. He was looking at the debris cloud of all that remained. Their ride was gone. All twelve members of its crew were dead, leaving them stranded on this dead world. Suddenly, his mind raced once more. Who would benefit from what occurred? Initially, it appeared that the imesht were the prime benefactors in this situation. But this latest development spoke of deeper involvement. Kendell couldn't account for how swiftly Bran knew of the incident and the imesht observer's appointment. At the same time, thoughts of the shuttle's fuel and supply limitations wrestled with the inevitable result of landing on the damaged world.

"Kendell. Kendell!"

The helanx repeated his name. He shook his head to clear it and turned to look at Tunegura.

"What do you know about the Diversiform Disputes?"

The question seemed so off-topic, it brought all his colliding worries to a halt. "Just the basics," he stammered.

"Available worlds are competed for in contests where the species involved in the Disputes develop a complete ecosystem for the world. The environment must sustain at least five other galactic species. The most effective system is awarded the world for development."

"What does that have to do with all of this?" he cried and then grew silent as the elements of the puzzle came into focus. "The imesht. The imesht are poor participants in this system, aren't they? Not only that, but they could sell humanity's improved terra-forming methods to other galactics and then have them ensure the environments created are hospitable to the imesht. They must have bought out Bran. They put this whole thing together. You have it, don't you? Proof of the signal?"

"Yes," Tunegura replied. "Proof that the imesht were trying to blackmail your species using the errors of its past."

Kendell stared at the helanx in shock.

"One of the things that most species forget about the helanx is that we are very adaptable, as well as mechanically inclined. We can survive on most worlds designed by the species of the Galactic Community."

"And that makes you excellent observers."

"Well put, Kendell. Now, as an official representative of the Community, I need to ask you a very important question in consideration of the recent events. What will you do about the terra-forming information that the imesht are seeking?"

Slumping back into the seat, Kendall thought, *What could he do?* Bran would stick to his deal with the imesht to sell out humanity. *Wait*, his mind must be moving slower than normal. "You have another ship waiting to pick us up," he fired off, pointing at the helanx.

"True, but not important. What will you do?"

"Just a few hours ago, I told the imesht that I could not speak for Governance, now you want me to make a decision that will affect all of humanity. What makes you think that I have the right?"

"You are in a unique position to do something that will show your species' commitment to the Galactic Community. It doesn't take a mandate to do that."

"Deep down, I know you are right. What can do we do?" He stopped for a moment, his breath catching at the audacity of the idea occurring to him. "We broadcast the terra-forming techniques as a gift to the Community as a whole."

"You do realize that this may eventually lead to the revelation of your past?"

Looking at the images projected in front of him, the barren, scoured rock and ceaseless winds tore at Kendall. "We've hidden it for too long. We've held on to this technology with no place to use it because we aren't competing in the Disputes." *We should have used it here*, he thought. Then he rounded on Tunegura once more. "If we do this, we should have the right to compete in the Diversiform Disputes."

Tunegura stated, "Do you, as a representative of the Human Governance, offer the terra-forming technologies to the Galactic Community as a whole?"

"I do," Kendell replied.

"You have helped your species take another step toward inclusion into the greater Community. Your worlds will be welcome to compete in the Disputes. As a consideration of your efforts to uncover the plot by the imesht, I will ensure that humanity will also receive help from the Galactic Community that will increase the efficiency of your transition ships."

"But why?"

"Because you have proved yourself worthy, as a species. And as a representative, you have proved that you can make the right choice for the greater good of the whole, a galactic whole, instead of for purely personal or species gain."

Kendell sighed. All the tension ran out of his body. Sprawling back in his seat, he looked again at the ground below them. "Maybe one day, we can do the right thing and use what we now know to correct our mistake. One day we can welcome your kind here as a visitor."

The helanx spun its wheel briefly. "You can welcome all of us."

A Talent Beyond My Talents

Avalem came to the Pillar of Night when his art failed him for what he decided was the last time. Looking upward at the vast cylinder that blotted out the sun and cast its shadow across the lands to the east, he forced himself to admit his ability had not always failed him. Second thoughts gnawed at him as he tried to make a case for all the things he remained good at: painting, illuminating, drawing, writing. But overall, he was just *good* at these. He would never excel at any of them, and no one wanted to pay for just good when it came to art. *Might as well paint a barn or do accounting or drafting,* Avalem thought. *I know I was meant for more.* So, when his latest commission failed to live up to his patron's expectation, Avalem left. He turned toward the east and walked across the lands until he came to the Pillar of Night.

The stories said much about the Pillar: the Long-Chain-Makers left it when they fled Earth; hollow, it went up so high that no air remained at its peak; and that people lived inside of it.

But those were not the stories that brought Avalem here. The Greal story moved him inexorably to the Pillar of Night. A strange thing that could imbue a man with a talent beyond his current abilities. He'd seen some of the art made by the Greal-touched and it amazed him. A depth to every piece that seemed to transcend what a mere man could create. Such pieces were priceless, and collectors of fine works fought like feral dogs over them. So, Avalem came for the Greal, to step beyond what he was, no matter the price.

The closer Avalem approached, the less of the sky he could see until the Pillar stood like a vast silvery wall covered in dark gray veins. He shook his head in amazement.

According to legend, in the last days of their leaving, the Long-Chain-Makers grew the Pillar and launched themselves from its peak. They built the tesseract out of the Moon, its eerie emanations only visible overhead at night. Like divers, they jumped from the edge of the solar system to swim for other stars. They went out amongst the other worlds and rearranged things to their liking. *One of these days,* he thought, *others will tell stories just as fantastic about me.*

A well-worn path led him onward into the valley. At the lowest point lay the entrance to a tunnel. Just inside that tunnel, as the light began to fade, someone stepped forward and laid a hand on his chest, bringing him to a halt.

"How you planning on seeing, boy?" came a rough voice. A tiny light appeared beside the face of a gray-haired man.

Avalem started and stepped backward. It hadn't occurred to him that the Pillar of Night would be completely dark. An opening at the top allowed some light to get in. Of course, he hadn't planned on the tunnel either. The man looked at him with a bit of a grin and offered, "Could sell you this here light if you need it."

He handed the strange lamp to Avalem. The loop of glass tube contained one small bright point of light. The light bobbed about as Avalem tilted the tube.

"Gonna' play with it or buy it?" barked the seller, his arms crossed over his chest.

"A fiscum," Avalem offered, turning the light about again.

"Two, that's final."

"Done." The man grabbed the silvers from Avalem's palm and turned to go into the darkness.

Without thinking, Avalem asked, "Don't you need a lamp?" Looking at the lamp merchant, he realized there were several of the tubes tied together on the man's back, all of which glowed. The merchant's eyes flashed in the half-light, gleamed like an animal's outside of a fire circle.

"Do I look like I need a lamp?" The merchant's footsteps faded into the darkness. Then Avalem heard him exclaim in the distance, "Don't forget to tell it you love it!"

Crazy old man, Avalem thought, starting down the path once more. When he held the lamp out to the side, he could barely see anything in the darkness. There were no walls nearby, and the ceiling hung invisible overhead. Occasional drops of water fell on him, and the ground felt rough and uneven. Avalem kept on walking.

At first, he thought the light became dimmer with each step. Then the lamp went out, the bright point fading away. Shaking the tube of glass produced nothing. The lamp seller tricked him.

The darkness closed in around Avalem, and his breathing grew hoarse. He would be trapped here at the mercy of the strange inhabitants of the foothills who could see in the dark. With some trepidation, he cleared his throat and said, "I love you." The spark grew to a globe the size of a grape and gave off a soft, lambent light. It made no sense, but looking at the light source again, he said, "I love you. I love you." In his own mind, he realized that he loved the fact that it was no longer dark, and he no longer felt afraid. The spark of light before him grew into a white-hot sphere that pushed at the confines of the glass tube. Avalem grasped the tube using the edges of his cloak to keep his hands from burning. Then he turned back to the path.

He couldn't determine the point at which he entered the Pillar of Night. A small amount of ambient light caught his attention. As his eyes grew used to having something to lock onto, Avalem thrust the lamp under the edge of his cloak. The land around him glowed in an unexpected reddish radiance. He could see a body of water ahead that shone with a crimson aura illuminating its depths. The grass under his feet looked black with a single stripe of glowing incarnadine down the spine of its shaft. Trees were dark forms that loomed upward. The country of Night was nothing like he expected.

He took several steps and then pitched forward, tripping over a rock he had not seen. Avalem pulled out the lamp once more. It would mark him as a stranger here, but the alternative was to stumble through the darkness and hope his eyes would adapt. He made good time walking a game trail along the edges of a wood. Several deer, their eyes blazing golden reflections, bounded out ahead of him and crashed through the underbrush. He stole another look at the heavens. Did the pinpoint of light he could see overhead grow dimmer? A few steps further, and he felt certain. *Night in this country would mean absolute darkness,* he thought as he made his way into the woods.

Finding a fir tree, Avalem cut down several low limbs and made himself a bower. Wrapping his cloak about him, he did his best to get comfortable. Perhaps it was the darkness, but he dropped off to sleep despite his strange surroundings without any hesitation.

He woke to a dim flickering lamp. Swiftly, he renewed his vow to it, and just as he said the word "love," it brightened once again. Gathering his belongings, Avalem left his sleeping place, resuming his quest. He continued onward as the land dipped down. Forty miles from one side to the other, the land of The Pillar of Night lay before him, and his goal was the sinking well at its center. When he stepped into a stream, it occurred to Avalem that now he had a guide. Follow the water down to the center of the country of Night and he would arrive.

Walking along, he lost any concept of time. He could see better now. Perhaps his eyes were adapting. There were no homes or buildings along the side of the stream as he trudged on. Silvery white fish with huge bulbous eyes swam upstream against the current. He found their motion disturbing and odd. Avalem hoped his food would hold out until he left the Pillar once again.

The land continued to slope downward. Down and down, he went, scrambling over half-seen rocks as he followed the water. The sound of it running and gurgling filled his ears. It kept his mind off of what might be wandering the forest unseen about him. After a time, he saw a glow of red below him as the forest pulled back away from the stream.

When he scrambled over the last rock, Avalem set the lamp down for a moment. The stream flowed across a plain until it came to a lake that glowed with red light. There were copses of trees here and there and large rocks that dotted the flat land. Glancing up, he saw what looked like a slender thread that hung down from the darkness overhead. White at its center, the light from the outside faded to red and then to darkness. Underneath lay the lake, and it glowed with reflected luminance. *This is my destination*, he told himself. He picked up the lamp and started eagerly out onto the plain.

Standing on the shore of the lake, his hands and cloak painted red with the reflected light, Avalem breathed a sigh of satisfaction. *I am here. At last, I am here.* He shrugged off his cloak and dropped his satchel on the shoreline. Beside the source of the Greal, he hesitated, unsure of how to proceed.

Hearing a footfall, he turned to discover a group of men had come up behind him.

"You have no idea what to do next. Do you, boy?" The group's largest member strode forward. He held a stout walking staff tucked up under his arm. Turning back to the others, he continued, "They spend all their time trying to get here and then never have a clue what's next." This brought a chuckle from the other dozen men. The staff bearer turned back to Avalem. "Well, if you have no idea, I have a suggestion." The staff came out from under his arm, its end swinging around in an arc that ended against Avalem's head.

Staggering backward into the lake, Avalem threw up his hands to ward off another attack. Swinging the weapon over his head, Avalem's attacker ducked in for another jab, knocking Avalem onto his back and into the water.

Feeling his feet slip out beneath him, Avalem kicked feebly in the water and then slid under the surface. Flailing about in the red darkness of the lake, he hit bottom and pushed himself back up again. Taking shuddering breaths, Avalem lurched out of the lake. His attacker looked up from the contents of Avalem's satchel. "Still haven't figured it out, have you?" the man growled, his hands tightening on the staff once more. Avalem crouched down in the reeds and balled his fists, anticipating another strike. The leader of the band feinted once toward Avalem's head and then swung the end of the staff around hard into his victim's stomach. The air burst from Avalem. He teetered on his heels for a moment, his belly lurching in pain. The red light wheeled overhead, and a rushing sound filled his ears. He wasn't breathing. Knees buckling, Avalem pitched forward. Just before he hit the water, he pulled in a ragged breath and heard from his assailant. "You've gotta drink it, boy, drink it deep." Then Avalem plunged into the lake, its cold water cascading down his throat.

Reddish light exploded behind his eyes and in the water about him. He felt himself strike bottom. The water he'd breathed in came choking out, and more water slid into his mouth and up his nose. His feet slipped, and his hands sank into the mud. *I'm going to die here*, he thought. Flailing his arms about, he pushed himself away from the mud. For a moment, he lost the surface. So little light fell into the depths and then diffused throughout the lake. In his confusion, Avalem pushed out his legs and arms, seeking any contact. He felt a grip settle around his ankle, pulling him from the lake. As soon as his head broke the water, Avalem spit up the remaining water. Soaking wet and shivering, he clung to the shoreline. Something blocked out the red light, and he drew back, still gasping in air.

"Welcome to Night, boy. Hope you found what you were looking for. Thanks for all the goods. Won't be seeing you again."

The owner of the voice strode off into the dark, his footfalls diminishing. Avalem felt his awareness start to fade. The light in front of his eyes wavered. He pulled at the reeds around him, trying to draw himself from the water before losing consciousness. He dragged his feet over the rocks of the shoreline and then curled into a shivering ball.

Avalem expected anything but warmth upon awakening. Clean blankets and sheets covered his nakedness. As he pulled himself into a sitting position, memories of almost drowning made him twitch.

Inside a room with minimal light, fibers drooped from the ceiling like fishing nets. Thick strands of material draped over everything in the room, covering a chair, a loom, a spinning wheel, and a wardrobe. A small window, shrouded as if wrapped in cobwebs, let in a tiny amount of light. He lay on the floor, he realized, wrapped in a nest of blankets. Pulling one around his hips, he climbed to his feet. Ducking low to avoid the hanging strands, he walked through the small, dim room to the doorway. The next room was larger, the ceiling again lost in fibrous netting. But he estimated this room, which looked to be the main one of the house, to be at least two stories tall.

He held his hand in front of his face for a moment. Even in the dimness of the room, he could see the lines on his palms. Blinking, he looked again. He knew his hands. He used them all the time in his work. Why did they look different now? Did the fingers look longer? Certain the lines were not where he remembered. Even his arms felt awkward, as though his forearms were too long and didn't fit. A rustling sound from overhead pulled him away from his observations. Looking up, he saw a graceful pair of legs push through the overhanging strands. The rest of the woman who followed was lithe and slim. She smiled at him for a moment and then, touching down on the floor, turned away to the other side of the room. Stopping, she looked over her shoulder and said, "I am very glad to find you better. Please come and break your fast with me."

Avalem followed her into yet another chamber lit by several of the strange lights like his lost lamp. His hostess touched each in passing, and the illumination within grew brighter. In the increased light, Avalem noticed the woman's strange garment. From some angles, it appeared to be a short dress, but as she turned, he could see that more of her legs were covered than he remembered. Stumbling a bit over the sheet wrapped about his hips, he then noticed her one bare shoulder and how the dress gathered up at one thigh. Looking away and then back, he found that her clothing altered yet again. The fabric was constantly in motion, individual strands sliding to and fro in an unsettling manner.

So instead, he focused on her face, its slim lines set into a knowing smile. She pushed her long red hair over one shoulder, and he saw something in the line of her back that made him want to look twice, but she turned away, pulling fruit from a cabinet and placing it in woven baskets that were on a low table that sat along one wall. She drew a chair from the other side of the room and placed it next to the one at the table. "Please," she said, urging him to sit down. Avalem managed the feat without falling over but with little grace. A quick smile traced its way across her face as she joined him at the table.

His hostess revealed bread, apples, and other fruits. Despite the soreness of his throat, Avalem found himself quite hungry. She pushed the baskets across the top of the table in front of him and settled back to watch, her hands clutching a small cup of tea. Breaking off bread, he dipped it in a small dish of honey and paused after the first bite, eyes closed in enjoyment. Her short laugh caught him by surprise.

"It is good to see someone enjoy something so simple," she said, hiding her smile behind the teacup.

"I am quite in your debt for, well, for everything. Thank you for rescuing me." Avalem bowed his head briefly to his host.

She made a vague gesture with one hand, and the curtains on the nearby window parted.

"All sorts of things wash up here, and occasionally I take an interest." Her eyebrow flicked upward briefly as her smile grew more mischievous.

Suddenly very aware of his lack of dress, Avalem covered the awkward moment by reaching for his tea. The woman turned to gaze out the window, and once again, he caught a glimpse of something on her shoulder, close to the nape of her neck. Looking now, he discovered that her hair did not precisely fall in waves but was lifted by something that rose from her back.

"I am sorry to be rude. My name is Avalem. I should have told you that before."

"Interesting, but unnecessary. Out there, I am sure that you have a use for names so that you can bind things to your definitions. In here, we don't care much about what one calls anything. We care about what it really is and its potential."

Taken aback by that statement, Avalem paused with his tea halfway to his lips. "What do I call you?"

Her laugh rose sweet and brief as her gaze returned to the lake. "You can call me the Lady of the Lake, the Sorceress of the Night, the Greal Witch. I am the weaver, and I know every one of my threads and can feel all of them. You decide what to name me, I will know, no matter what, when you choose to call me."

Her head shot around, and she met his gaze as every thread in the entire house leapt through the air to connect with her. For an instant, she appeared a glorious spider lying at the heart of a web encompassing every portion of her house. Just as quickly, a ripple in the curtains by the window caught Avalem's attention, and the all-pervasive threads vanished.

He sat there for a moment, overwhelmed. Then cautiously, he said, "I think I shall just call you Lady."

One red eyebrow shot up, as well as the corners of her mouth, "Oh, foundling, you and I shall get along well."

When they were done with the meal, she found him trousers and a shirt made of the ever-present material that filled her home. When she led him out into the light, Avalem started to ask her why he could suddenly see, but she silenced him with a finger across his lips and pulled him down to the lake. They spent the afternoon walking along the sands of its shore. Reaching down, she cupped a handful of the lake's waters. Like a liquid ruby, the surface rippled with each of her breaths. "Do you know the story of the Long-Chain-Makers?" she asked.

"I know they remade the world and left."

"There is a great deal more. Years and years ago, men tried to make intelligences other than their own. They used tiny machines to weave great nets of logic, but it never occurred to them that the small ones would learn as they worked. Each one of the Chains is forged of links of makers, communers, and unmakers. They were made to be more than the sum of their parts, and they came together, becoming more than the whole."

Avalem looked up at the immensity of the interior of the Pillar of Night. "And they built this."

"Yes, and they also changed us. They left humanity with an extended lifespan, as well as the power to heal most injuries and to consume nearly anything. But the Long-Chain-Makers also built us a cage, taking away our ability to undo their alterations. They changed us so we can't survive anywhere but Earth. Then they took away all our toys, leaving us with just enough to get by. They founded a world where the works of one's hands and mind and the flavors we could enjoy became a new currency. The world became temperate and plentiful everywhere under their touch. Lastly, they also made the Greal. But even that is fading."

With that, she flicked her hair aside, and Avalem could clearly see the series of growths that ran up the back of her shapely neck like shelf fungus.

"In the beginning, merely a touch from the lake would have transformed you. Now those ruffians practically had to drown you before you took enough in."

"Do you mean... "

The Lady let her hair fall back once more with a laugh. "Don't be foolish. How could you see as well as you do if you hadn't changed?"

Avalem stepped away from her side and ran his fingers over the back of his neck. Then he stared intently at his hands.

"There's nothing yet. It's too early."

"What?" He took a deep breath, shaking with relief and astonishment that he was at last different from everyone else. "What can I do now?"

She threw her hands up in the air, a shower of scarlet water raining down. "Who knows? Each ability is unique."

Then she led him back toward the house, between the rows of sculptured shrubs that extended on either side and then back into the woods. They walked the corridors of the maze until she brought them to the center and the rose garden concealed there. A copper orrery whirled about from nothing but the air of their passing. Scattered about were works of art clearly fashioned by the Greal-touched. A tree shaped into a mermaid leaping from the spray, and yet overhead, its foliage gave them shade. A granite rock braided like hair. Each nook and alcove hid another treasure. Avalem remained bemused at the variety of the wonders as the Lady led him to a marble bench.

"They are presents from those who have found their aspect of the gift the Greal bestowed on them."

"Finally," Avalem sighed, convinced that at last his life had changed for the better.

The Lady reached out and laid her hand against his cheek. "What you will do will be amazing no matter where your talent lies. But there are some who cannot learn to master their abilities and others who fall under the influence of the unscrupulous. I do my best to teach them, but you've seen how others react to what the Greal-touched make."

Indeed, thought Avalem, briefly unable to meet her gaze.

The Lady continued, "What you have is like a hammer. It can be used to build an edifice of towering beauty, or it can be swung with murderous intent. We'll find out together."

"Then I'll give you a gift that will make all of these other gifts pale in comparison."

Her smile took him by surprise, so too the warm, twining fingers among his own. Together they walked hand and hand back to the house. There she stroked the closest lamp into light.

"Why does that work?" Avalem asked.

"It's a talent, a Greal-given talent."

"You mean the man in the tunnel... " It did explain the other's ability to see in the dark. "But the 'I love you'?"

The Lady ran her fingers across the top of the glass and the light within chased after their tips. "It's a maker, a maker of light. It works because we want it to, and it can actually sense intent. Therefore, we need to prove we need its light."

"But—"

Her smile stopped him. "Love is a word we don't say often." A brief awkward silence reigned until the Lady finally broke it. "Hungry?"

Lady kept casting him glances through the curtain of her hair, which fell forward in a fetching way throughout dinner. As the light faded in the window across the table, Avalem found no surprise after the incidental touches throughout their meal that once again she reached for his hand and drew him further into the house. She pulled him onward, the webbing of her home growing deeper, the fabric of his clothes rustling on their own. Her clothing unwove itself before his eyes, revealing more and more of her milk-white skin. When she drew her hands to him, he felt his own shirt and pants slough away and rejoin the mass of threads about them. Threads swept under their feet, and buoyed them up, and wove them into a vast cocoon that sealed out the world. Then, like the giant web that it was, all the strands in the house began to sway with the gentle motion their joining imparted.

When Avalem awoke in the darkness due to nature's need, he wondered briefly how he might find his way down to the floor. The nest reacted to his turning and unknitted itself in such a way allowing him to exit their bower without disturbing the Lady. He looked back and found himself bemused by her splayed form, the fall of her breasts, and the way that her tresses merged with the strands of the net.

She turned, and her shoulder came into view, the design that broke its alabaster skin drawing his attention back. A rose raised itself above the surface of her skin. A filigree of woven skin lay across its stem and petals, holding it in place. The stem grew from the Lady's skin at the base, and several of the petals on the underside of the flower were also joined to her. Shock filled him, and, for a moment only, she breathed. Staring at his hands, the inevitable revelation came: *I have done this.*

Avalem fled.

Whipping strands from his path, he found his way back to the room where he first awoke and threw open the closets there until he discovered most of his clothes. Beneath them also lay his satchel and the lamp. For an instant, he fell further into shock. Why would the Lady have these things? Could she have recovered them from the pack of ruffians? Or had she actually ordered them to cast him into the lake?

No matter how hard he looked, he could not find his shirt, but in another closet lay one made of the Lady's material. His hands shook as he drew on her shirt. He gathered up his belongings, sliding once more through the webbing, fearing to signal the spider at its heart of his departure. Caught between the elation of discovery and the fear of how she might react to what he had done to her, he felt confused. In this state of mind, he could only think to run. When he finally cleared the doorway, Avalem breathed a sigh of relief.

Walking through the forest, returning to the entry tunnel, he once again considered the surface of his hands. Was there more detail to the lines that traced his palms? How could these ordinary parts of him that he had known and used all these years have accomplished what he'd discovered? All artists used their hands; where else could he have imagined the Greal coming from to work such a transformation? But what could he do with a talent like this? Could he be worse off than before he came? Avalem's head sank forward as he continued to trudge along. Changed forever, but who could say if such a change was for the best. He passed into the tunnel and left the Land of Night.

A week later, he came upon a girl drawing in the dirt, her left arm hanging limply by her side. Her infirmity drew him despite himself.

Once the Pillar of Night had become a smudge in the distance, he'd deliberately avoided villages. Going out of his way to stay clear of others had become the norm. The back of his neck filled with strange bumps that grew day by day, and his hands itched incessantly. At night, he forced them into his satchel, drawing the string tight with his teeth. Several times, he'd blanked out and discovered himself with his arm plunged into the ice-cold streams of the area. *Something is wrong with me.* He couldn't understand it. He couldn't explain why he'd come here.

Now Avalem stumbled up to the girl, reaching for her dragging limb. Some part of his awareness felt bemused by the damage to her arm. The gifts of the Long-Chain-Makers altered human physiology so that such a break should easily heal, but something must have gone wrong. His fingers touched her arm, and in that instant, all the confusion and the irritation in his fingers passed away.

She had a moment to look up at him confused before the Greal acted, and then its insidious strength poured into her, reworking the very nature and stuff of her limb. The Greal flicked through possibilities until settling on an answer. Then a wave of heat cascaded from his reworked digits, both making and unmaking at the same time. The end result gave him a brief sense of satisfaction that he later attributed to the Greal and then a growing sense of horror at what he'd done. This stranger, whom he'd never met nor spoken to, now had a new arm. This limb was a helical weaving filled with spiraling filigrees whose bones and joints were refashioned into not only an efficient but also elegant form. The skin wove over the entire construct but not so densely as to hide the new architecture within. Avalem had never seen anything like it. He'd taken her broken arm and made it into a work of art. Maybe, just maybe, his talent did have value.

He had only that moment to admire his work before a man grasped his shoulder and threw him to the ground.

While Avalem lay there staring at the hulking figure that reached for the long curved threshing blade that hung at his waist, he felt the need rising from the Greal once more. It wanted. It wanted him to lay hands on this other, to remake him, to string the sinew differently, reorganize the skin and weave bone into something amazing. The sensation overwhelmed him, and he did not move quickly enough to stop the stranger from lopping the arm from the girl.

Shock overwhelmed Avalem. Instinctively, he knew that the arm would grow back, that it should be straight and whole once more. It reminded him of the beating he'd received at the side of the lake in the Pillar of Night. Mankind's bodies were designed to take so much more punishment now that it was very difficult to truly hurt one another. However, the Greal-influenced part of him also wondered in what state the limb would return. The natural repair systems of her body must have failed before leaving her with a useless limb. Avalem had just enough time to observe that her bleeding stopped immediately, and the skin of her back stretched to cover the missing area before her assailant turned on him.

"Whatever you did to my daughter, I won't stand for it. She'll have a perfectly good arm now, not that abomination you created. We were only waiting until she could accept what had to be done until you stepped in."

The blade turned toward him, and Avalem caught the other man's wrist with both hands, once again feeling the slippery hot sensation of the Greal at work. The makers inside of him evaluated the wrist and remade it even as he turned the blow away. The metal of the scythe, also raw material, reappeared as part of the resulting architecture. A well-intentioned mistake played out against him. For now, the farmer turned his wrist in an impossible fashion and captured both of Avalem's. The rewoven mesh of metal and flesh making the grip inexorable. The girl's father gave a long wail of frustration and cried out, "Help me!"

Then Avalem felt the first blow strike his head, and others fell about his shoulders as the villagers came to their comrade's rescue using the handles of their farming implements as weapons. Avalem's body desperately tried to keep him conscious, and he could feel the Greal at work here and there when another came within his grasp. Finally, as he curled in upon himself on the ground, he felt his awareness slipping away.

When he awoke, Avalem found himself inside a small conical granary. The door blocked, the only light coming in through chinks in the gaps between the masonry. When he stood up, his shoulders brushed the sides of the enclosure. The heat and the grain dust were stifling. Worse still, the itching in his hands had begun again. The Greal anxious once again to alter flesh after he'd finally used his talent. Sitting down, he wrapped his hands in his shirt. He wasn't sure when he started, but Avalem began to rock back and forth. The heat surrounding him grew as the sun rose farther into the sky. Emanations from the Greal grew more and more intense. The walls wavered in his vision. The granary a forge as he felt himself being cast anew.

The Lady followed Avalem. Once again, she touched the rose, now forever a part of her. Something drew her forth from the safety of Night—the material of his shirt calling to her. But its song grew weaker when she arose in the morning and rapidly faded away. Still, she suspected she would not have to look any farther than the village that lay in the valley below her. When she walked down its central road, a small crowd of children flowed about her on either side, noisily playing with strange toys. Mechanical birds sang sweetly, flying creations spun of their own accord, lifting into the air, musical instruments, and more. From each, the Lady felt the vague echo of her work. When she looked carefully, the parts seemed to be carved from ivory or bone and bound with tanned thongs. Beyond the children, the men and women of the village picked through a bounty of knives, tools, and baskets, all strewn about the remains of the last of three granary towers.

Possibilities flashed through her mind. The Lady knew that Avalem was here, all about her now. The Greal remade him entirely, frustrated at its inability to act when the villagers locked him away. Unconsciously, she rubbed at the back of her neck. *But why*, she wondered. Then it came to her, a truth she had not expected. Avalem's Greal was a tool too valuable to be wasted. For the first time in untold years, something free in the world could undo the very chains that bound humanity to Earth. Because it could alter human physiology, Avalem's Greal could reverse the changes made by the Long-Chain-Makers. She felt a certainty that each and every piece that resulted from his transubstantiation bore the Greal to its new owner. More than likely, a new version of the Greal, better tempered and less likely to consume its host. The ability would spread from person to person, a plague of possibilities where before there were none.

The Lady's hand came to rest on the rose again as she remembered waking the previous night and staring up at the stars. In the Pillar of Night, she'd long since forgotten the simple joy of considering their multitudes. What wonders now awaited them out there? At last, they could walk the path that the Long-Chain-Makers had laid ages ago. However, a long way remained to go before humanity could leave Earth, but each journey begins with a single step. She knelt and reached out for the nearest toy. The puzzle box slowly unfolded under her inquisitive fingers; the rose hidden at its heart no surprise at all.

BLANKETS

COLLATERAL DAMAGE, KIERSEY THOUGHT, STARING AT THE SMALL, sandaled foot as he pulled more branches off of the body. That's what Lieutenant Roberts would call it, but all Kiersey saw was a young boy who should be running and playing. Their medic, Leigh, looked over the casualty quickly and logged the cause of death as exposure. She took a blood sample for confirmation because Leigh was nothing if not diligent. If the exploratory force from the *Ross* weren't planetside, the kid at his feet might still be alive.

Kiersey cut himself off. *Time to rein it in and focus on the task at hand,* he thought.

"Eyes ahead, Kiersey. No way you get to keep looking at my ass."

Shaking his head, Kiersey stopped his impromptu burial to stare at Bangs. She wasn't just all talk; she had a bad habit of acting out of hand as well. Taking her LinAcc rifle in one hand, she proceeded to wriggle suggestively. In a motion almost too fast to see, Bangs dropped the rifle into her cradling hands and whipped around so that its bore faced Kiersey for a second before it swung away.

"Bangs!" Roberts's voice cut through the comm. "Get on point and cut it."

She looked at Kiersey a moment longer, shouldered her weapon, then slapped her ass before moving ahead. Shaking his head, Kiersey turned away from her antics. Tapping the contact plate on his temple twice, he brought up the enhancement and overlay to his vision. He pushed the viewpoint up and out until he could see the team high-lighted in ghostly blue throughout the valley floor. The Mosquito.net system of microaerosats that he'd deployed spread and increased their coverage. Each one of the team had an aerosat shadowing them, and Kiersey could view any individual. More importantly, so could Roberts. To his left, Anderev flanked Kiersey while Breadle and Peake brought up the rear. Heyer and Michaels ranged to the right, and Roberts stayed to the center.

"Move out," came Roberts' order.

Pulling the viewpoint even higher, Kiersey looked over the terrain. The team worked its way up the valley toward the highest point in the area and the targeted lookout emplacement. One valley over, the secondary team moved slower, keeping to the hedgerows and avoiding the open areas of the tilled fields.

Kiersey continued to spread the net, carefully maintaining a cautious overlap of each of the aerosat elements. Everyone had their specialties, and this was his. He felt a brief jab of satisfaction at the way he performed as the commtech.

While he'd listened earlier to Roberts's impassioned briefing about the necessity of securing Cansec, the Sylvan Seven world of their current assignment, Kiersey had trouble squaring what they were told with the limited amount of resistance the team encountered. Where were the dangerous rebels that Roberts warned them about? The *Ross* dropped teams now for two weeks, and they'd encountered little resistance. The thought hit him. He'd served in enough action on heavily colonized worlds to know that the boy he'd buried could have easily carried a sizeable explosive device into a trusting company and wreaked havoc. But everything Kiersey saw pointed to someone who'd wandered out into the woods and died of natural causes. He tried to focus on that.

Anderev's hand on his shoulder brought him back into focus. Blinking, Kiersey readjusted his vision and nodded at the veteran combat specialist. With two fingers, Anderev gestured him forward and then loped off to the left, resuming his position. The valley turned, and now Kiersey could see the rise ahead. He pushed several Mosquito.net 'sats ahead of them toward the target, keeping them high and spread wide. The group of 'sats pinged him back—one kilometer ahead, there were three IR sources that bore metallic returns moving toward the team.

Kiersey flipped the info over to Roberts, and the lieutenant called Bangs to a halt, sending the flankers ahead. Moments later, weapon fire tore through the quiet tree-covered hillsides of the valley.

Transcript of Committee Hearing, Sylvan Seven Atrocities

General Pressman: The war stalled. We were unable to continue to promote an effective campaign against the renegade worlds. The systems, which were dependent upon the support of the renegades and were within reach, recaptured, and opposition quelled. The remaining seven worlds continued to resist. We had the troop carriers, the troops, and the desire to finish the conflict, but we no longer had the backing or the finances. We were not given the option to stop the conflict.

Senator Wellheim: I'm sorry, general, maybe I misunderstood. You told me you couldn't continue.

General Pressman: Under traditional methods, we had no means of an assured victory.

Senator Wellheim: You seem to be implying that you considered alternatives: alternatives that perhaps were outside of Article II of the Geneva Protocols.

General Pressman: I'm stating a fact. Implying nothing. You already know what we did. You just need to hear me say it. It will go quicker, be more efficient, and cost less overall if you do not interrupt.

There were several radical ideas proposed, most of which were summarily dismissed. The final solution depended upon the fact the selected troop carriers were prepared to make the nadir transition to return from the fringe to the central stars, and that redeployment would take an unacceptable amount of time and cost. Given that each nadir jump takes four objective years and one year subjective time, the task force of seven ships was twelve years out. All ships were contacted, new orders were issued, and the task force turned about.

Senator Wellheim: Let me stop you there, general. Your use of the word contact is a bit of a euphemism, isn't it?

General Pressman: The ships' military-class AI's were contacted and given new orders, which were not revealed to the human complement.

Senator Wellheim: Wasn't one of those orders to ensure the failure of the refueling drones?

General Pressman: We made sure that what was necessary was done.

Senator Wellheim: You are content with the result?

General Pressman: We achieved the reacquisition of the colonies. That is the only result that matters.

"What the hell was that? What kind of idiot makes that much noise?" Peake asked over the comm.

Kiersey swung his bar-buster around at the sounds from ahead. He snugged his helmet down on his head, his fingers briefly catching on the hanger hook attached to the back. The rectangular bar-buster hummed in his hands when the weapon's field went live. His gun had limited accuracy, but the amount of ammunition it could sling made up for that failing. As the hostile fire ahead started up again, Kiersey realized what bothered Peake. All the combat team's weapons were silent until impact. The older-style slug throwers made a racket and gave away their user's positions. When Kiersey looked at the view from the net, he realized there were no IR spikes in the area that matched the trajectories of the enemy fire.

Sweeping his view over the team, he found Breadle down and Peake standing next to his fallen comrade, firing his bar-buster. Breadle rolled over onto his side, trying to get up on one knee. Roberts received all the feed and made the intuitive jump before Kiersey did, redirecting the fire from Peake and Anderev up into the canopy of the trees. As lucky as ever, Bangs crouched untouched behind the stump of a toppled tree, her LinAcc pointed toward the incoming hostiles. Kiersey picked them out, painted them, and passed the info along to Roberts. Seconds later, the first one slumped forward, promptly followed by the next. The final combatant turned to make a run for it, but Bangs's headshot brought his limp form to the ground.

Kiersey fanned out the aerosats, looking for more movement. Then he caught an image from Anderev and quickly forwarded it to Roberts—the fire the combat group received came from two automated systems embedded in the trunks of large trees.

At the base of the nearest tree, Heyer looked up at the splintered remains. "Why the hell do that?"

"The tree covered up the metallic ping and soaked up the heat signature. It's high enough to give the system good covering fire, and lastly, a bunch of farmers don't think like we do." Anderev's delivered his assessment in a clipped tone.

"Too right. Only a bunch of farmers could figure on kicking the Federate and not expect a response," returned Bangs as she got to her feet.

Kiersey began a broad sweep looking for any emission from more emplacements, resetting the parameters to catch the limited exposure of the embedded traps. Roberts turned his attention to Bangs's feed, and Kiersey found himself following along using the 'sat that shadowed her. She crept up on the casualties and then came to an abrupt halt.

"What is it, Bangs?" Roberts sent.

When she turned, the body at her left came into view. At first, all that Kiersey could see were the muddy boots and non-mutable camouflage, then Bangs walked closer. The cylinders strapped to the dead man's face were unmistakable.

"Go to BW-1. All team, BW-1. Now," Roberts barked over the comm.

Bangs's chatter reduced to a constant stream of profanity that Kiersey chopped off. Her shoulders shook once, then she reached around and pulled the filter clasp across the front of her helmet like they all were doing. Then her LinAcc came back up, and she straightened. He'd seen Bangs like this before. Someone was going to die and soon. He was just glad she was in front of him. Kiersey dialed back his viewpoint, and a twitch raced up his spine. Who knew what bioweapon they were all exposed to?

⁂

TRANSCRIPT OF COMMITTEE HEARING, SYLVAN SEVEN ATROCITIES

Senator Wellheim: Correct me if I'm wrong, general, but I understand that you gave your troops something extra.

General Pressman: All troops were inoculated with a new full-spectrum antigen.

Senator Wellheim: Well, that makes sense; you don't want your troops coming down with anything once they are groundside.

Leigh patched up as much of Breadle's side as she could while Kiersey and Peake watched over her. Kiersey stole a glance at Roberts. From his tense stance, the lieutenant was having a heated encrypted conversation with command onboard the *Ross*. Once Roberts secured evac for Breadle, Kiersey saw him send Peake to help the injured man to a clear LZ. Pushing the net farther, Kiersey kept scanning for enemy signatures. Now that he had a template from the automated guns in the trees, he identified two other emplacements. He caught Roberts's comm lighting up.

"Leigh," Roberts sent, and the medic jogged over to him. "I need a report, and I need it yesterday. What the hell did we just step in? How bad is it?"

Leigh looked away briefly. "Sir, I'm not certain what we're up against, but it's fairly virulent. When I knew that we were looking for a pathogen, something that I found from the casualty we discovered earlier made better sense. The boy shouldn't have died from exposure. It just doesn't get cold enough during this season. His cause of death must be due to whatever the rebels released. I'm still trying to narrow it down, but there were some unusual viruses in his system."

"Are we safe?" Roberts asked.

"Our new antigen treatment should cover most of what the opposition could throw at us."

Roberts put a hand on Leigh's shoulder and turned her away from the team, their comm's chatter switching to encrypted. Kiersey considered what had just happened. Roberts wasn't very subtle when it came to communication. If Kiersey didn't know any better, he'd swear that the encryption slip was deliberate. He didn't get any time to think about it further because Roberts redeployed the team and once again started them toward the highest point. Kiersey could still hear Bangs mumbling under her breath as they struck out.

A body lay in the clearing at the base of the rise. The metal in the gun it held pinged on the Mosquito.net, but its temperature had dropped enough that the IR could not immediately discern it. After making their way around the two tree emplacements, the team continued on to the objective. At the foot of the hill, the trees were cut down to give the defenders on the heights the advantage of a clear line of sight. Except, when Kiersey flew the aerosats over the landscape, he found no IR spikes or metallic pings other than the fortified position on the hillside identified from orbit by the *Ross*. *Where are all the defenders?* he wondered.

Kiersey brought a group of aerosats level with the front of the opening in the hillside that led via a switchback tunnel up to the keep above them. Nothing. Still no heat signatures. Once inside, the 'sats found the bodies of two guards, one of them with his arms outstretched, futilely reaching for a cylinder mask. Beyond that, there were more dead, all of which were cold enough that Leigh couldn't even guess at a time of death.

"What the hell happened here?" Heyer mumbled.

Roberts stood, considering the scene before him. Kiersey watched him shake his head briefly. Then the lieutenant spoke, sending Bangs in to lead, followed by Heyer and Michaels. Kiersey looked at the 'sat readings again.

The cave ran straight back for fifty meters before starting to ascend. Roberts sent him a brief message, "Stay here with Anderev. Move some aerosats over our back trail and continue to push forward the ones in the cave." With that, the lieutenant motioned Leigh ahead of him toward the dead guards.

Kiersey picked a 'sat near Bangs and watched as she moved further into the cave. Still twitchy, her shoulders jerked back and forth. More bodies slumped against the sides of the cavern.

"This is bad," Michaels sent over the band. "It's like they didn't even know what they set loose."

"No chatter," Roberts replied from where he stood over Leigh as she examined the guard's body.

The furthest 'sat picked up an IR spike. Kiersey relayed the high-lighted view to the rest of the team. "You've got a live one all the way at the back of the cave. There are some metallic pings from around the combatant."

"Bangs!" Roberts sent, cutting across Kiersey, but she was already in motion, the LinAcc's barrel swinging in front of her as she tracked the enemy.

"What is this stuff?" came from Heyer, down on one knee in front of several bags made from coarsely spun fiber.

Roberts started to move away from Leigh. "Bangs, I need them alive. We need to know what's going on here."

"There's more over here. It's really fine," Michaels answered, something white and powdery spilled out onto the floor in front of him. "There's something buried under all of these bags. Look at the way they hump up in the middle."

Kiersey saw Anderev move in the corner of his eye. The combat specialist also watched the feed from the cave in a reduced window, according to Kiersey's log. A brief, sharp breath came from Bangs's feed, and a muffled thump as the LinAcc's ammunition found its target.

"Damn it, Bangs!" came from Roberts.

Kiersey flipped back to the feed from the 'sat shadowing Bangs just in time to see the thumb on her victim's hand rise.

In the cave, the team's audio caught the pop of small explosions. The 'sats images were overwhelmed by the fine white particles that shot into the air as the bags were destroyed. Kiersey's mind worked at putting everything he saw together when Anderev slammed into him, throwing them both to the ground. The feed from the 'sats vanished into bright-white overload. The ground shook momentarily, and an orange lance of fire jetted from the cave across the clearing into the surrounding woods. Kiersey felt himself rolling away from Anderev, his ears and eyes overwhelmed despite the protection of his helmet.

He came to rest on his back. Blinking his eyes, Kiersey looked upward in time to see a tree flying through the air. Its roots came down, striking him in the chest and shoving him along the ground for several meters.

A smell of something other than burning wood lingered when he came around. At the edges of Kiersey's awareness, he could hear Anderev muttering. He heard snatches of "Flour, of all things, damn primitives," and then "You're not going to like this, but I can't carry you." The burning scent got stronger, and when he dug far enough into his memory, Kiersey realized that it smelled just like incinerated flesh.

TRANSCRIPT OF COMMITTEE HEARING, SYLVAN SEVEN ATROCITIES

General Pressman: We gave our soldiers much more than just a new antigen.

Senator Wellheim: Enlighten us.

General Pressman: Ships by nature are very difficult to keep completely clean in a biological sense. They are breeding grounds for all kinds of new bacteria and phages, all altered by the incidence of cosmic rays and other radiations. By giving our crews the full-spectrum antibody, the infectious agents were encouraged to adapt, becoming more and more virulent over time. The soldiers, of course, would be fine.

Senator Wellheim: I note here on this report that the full-spectrum antibody does not necessarily destroy these hostile agents but rather stops any effect on the troops. General, do you have any response to that? No, I didn't expect you would.

This dream is really the worst, Kiersey thought as the feeling of floating continued. He had a few snatches of memory that kept coming back and made no sense. A disturbing tugging sensation, a release, and then a feeling like he sailed through the air as if he suddenly weighed nothing at all. It reminded him of the way the tree flew in the moments before landing on him. Then there were a few seconds of very distorted vision as if he were hanging upside down and swinging back and forth. Through all of this, he could smell that horrendous odor once again of burning flesh.

"OPS-AI, give him visual."

Kiersey worked over the new stimuli for a moment. *That's Anderev's voice,* he realized, and then he could see. The image before him wavered, and Kiersey recognized the infirmary onboard the *Ross.* He'd made it. He tried to turn his head in the direction that Anderev's voice came from, but nothing happened. The staff must have him secured, which made sense since he'd probably injured his back or neck. He heard a chair scrape on the flooring, and Anderev came into his line of sight.

The combat specialist was missing an arm. The slope of his shoulder cut off abruptly, and a reddish-blue bandage covered its absence. Burns colored what was visible of the rest of Anderev.

"It's not as bad as it looks, but when it itches, then it is that bad," Anderev grated out. "Sorry, smoke inhalation," he continued, pointing at his throat. "But what I'm really sorry about is that I couldn't carry you out... " his voice trailed off, and he looked away.

Kiersey felt briefly confused at that, thinking more clearly now than before. Perhaps they'd reduced the level of drugs in his system. "What do you mean?" His voice sounded tinny and unmodulated; perhaps he had some smoke inhalation damage as well.

Anderev didn't say anything for a moment. Then he reached across and pulled a slate off a nearby table. He fiddled with it awkwardly until its surface became reflective. "I'm not sure you're ready for this…" Again, he trailed off and then brought up the mirrored screen before Kiersey.

The rest of the room fell quiet while Kiersey went through several panicked reactions. But they were reactions that would have taken a body to act upon. His face was barely recognizable, and that was what remained of most of him. Just below his Adam's apple, Kiersey became a ragged mass of flesh. His body was gone. A gelatinous mass of blue, a tangle of tubes, and several flexing bellows were attached to his pitiful remains. His mind… his mind, however, continued to work. *Six long months, six incredibly long months, and the techs on the* Ross *will grow me a new body. I'll be more than just a chunk of flesh again.* Then he realized that Anderev remained much too quiet and still. "You saved my life," Kiersey said.

The big man's shoulders slumped. "About the only thing I saved," he sat down at the edge of Kiersey's vision.

"Now I know what you meant when you said you couldn't carry me." If he had a body, Kiersey would have shuddered. He'd heard before about the option of sealing the armor's helmet in life-threatening situations. But he'd never heard of anyone using it. The handle on the top of the helmet was not just for hanging it on the wall. Then he started to think more about what Anderev said.

"Look, we couldn't do anything for them. It happened so fast. I'm sure they never even felt it."

Anderev turned back around where Kiersey could see his face. Some of the tension there lessened. "Kiersey, you don't understand. All of those dead men and women down there, even that kid—it's all our fault."

"When we get sent in, people die. It's a fact."

Kiersey heard Anderev stand up to his feet. "No, you don't know. When we were sent down to Cansec, our hyped-up immune systems carried live, infectious agents. We were full of diseases that had to develop into radically dangerous forms as they tried to overwhelm our antigens, viruses that the population of that world had no protection from whatsoever."

As Anderev stepped out of Kiersey's line of sight, he heard him say softly, "Every last one of them is dead. We walked on their world, breathed its air, drank its water, and we *poisoned* them. We poisoned them so well that they never had a chance."

Kiersey heard Anderev's footsteps and then the *chuff* of the airlock door as it opened and closed. He stared at the opposite wall and its blank grey metal for a long time. Everything that he saw was a product of his imagination, and none of it could be as bad as the reality. "OPS," he said, "I think you can turn me off for a while. I think you can turn me off for a long while…"

TRANSCRIPT OF COMMITTEE HEARING, SYLVAN SEVEN ATROCITIES

Senator Wellheim: So, you knew full well what you were doing?

General Pressman: Sadly, sir, it is not without precedent. Our ancestors gave blankets impregnated with the smallpox infection to the Indians and achieved the same result. We did not arrive at our decision lightly. After all, it was a group of rebel farmers that started the American Revolution. Since the consolidation, the Federate simply is not prepared for another conflict. We were all aware of the consequences and accepted them as a necessary cost of winning this war.

Senator Wellheim: You condemned all those people to death.

General Pressman: No, sir, they accepted their fate when they challenged us. We were given little choice in how to accomplish our goal. I could just as easily lay the blame on your shoulders when your committee cut the finances to the war effort. But you do not want to see or hear that. You are only looking for someone to accept the blame. Well, I will. If you want to blame someone for accomplishing the goal that you tried to make certain could not be done, then blame me. If you want to blame someone for finishing this with no recourse, then blame me. If you want to blame someone for having the balls to do what it takes, then blame me. But don't you ever tell me that I have failed the Federal Coalition.

Senator, I'm done here. I have answered your questions. I have nothing further to say.

The Luminous Blind Spot

Cold air lanced through Perris's lungs as the traffic shrieked by on the nearby roadway. He spun to a halt as a snowflake lit on his eyelash. Time ended as if cut off. The world crunched down into a piece of reality less than a sixteenth of an inch across, one little water crystal unique among the millions that hung in the air overhead, ready to descend. So, in that fossilized now, James Perris spun to the left and collapsed over the banister.

Of the five senses, the one most commonly associated with memory is smell. When the air smelled familiar, it foreshadowed something. A milestone on the road to a destination, a road Perris had done everything possible to blockade—only to find himself racing down the black mnemonic highway once again with its inevitable destination…

The morning of Shawn's departure on her business venture for the biotech lab dawned, and Perris had spent the night. Over breakfast, he'd started feeling odd. One moment by moonlight, that perfect moment, he could run it back over and over again. In fact, he could run any memory from the previous night back and forth perfectly in exact detail, almost as if it could happen again in a collapsed version of time. He could recall any moment after they'd left the restaurant. When had his memory gotten that good? Putting a hand out to catch the cup of coffee he'd almost tried to hang in midair, Shawn said into the silence, "Actually, your memory was never that good, at least never as good as last night."

He swung around to stare at her, his mouth open, as she placed the cup on the tabletop and continued, "No, I'm not suddenly a mind reader—I just recognize the feeling and hence the expression."

Into the silence that followed, Perris dropped his head into his hands as his mind raced. One slightly off remark kept coming back to him, "Nice to see I'm not the only one who brings work home with them."

She'd given him something that they created in the lab, something to do with memory. *Oh, God, he was a human guinea pig.* He quickly squelched that reaction. Obviously, this was tested and nearly ready for release to the public. She loved him—she wouldn't put him at risk. Glancing up at her, he saw in an instant all he'd guessed was true.

"But do you know why?" she asked, looking him in the eye.

Perris pursed his lips. He had to admit, he didn't see an immediate reason, and then she caught him by surprise by leaning over and kissing him. Suddenly, echoes of multiple passionate kisses rocketed through his head. If he picked one, he could follow it through and re-live any one of several bouts of passionate lovemaking from the evening before. What a going away gift—a little memorable something to keep him going for two weeks.

"It only increases the extent of mnemonic absorption now for about ten hours. But the effects as far as we can tell are long-lasting."

"It's amazing," Perris said, unwillingly spiraling through a memory fragment of drinking coffee after dinner the evening before, brought on by the aroma of his current cup, which Shawn appropriated and now sipped. The wine, she'd slipped it into his second glass of wine, and he'd finished the coffee before they'd left to take the edge off of the wine. "But how?" he asked.

"Two things," she said, handing back the coffee. "One, it gets easier to control. It's like having a new sense you didn't even know you had, like memory discretion. Two, it would take about two months to ground you in enough theory to understand 'how,' and even then, I couldn't guarantee I could explain it all completely. But look, let's just say we added something to your neural paths called a mnemocyte, a sort of nanotech intermediary. It allows you to map your storage paths more efficiently. Sorry, that was all obviously a mouthful of vague complexities. Okay, what's four plus three?"

"Seven," Perris replied.

"Two plus five?"

"Seven."

"One plus six?"

"Seven."

"Nine minus two?"

"Seven. Look, somewhere along here there is a point, right?" Perris snapped finally.

"Yes, but bear with me, what vegetable comes to mind?"

"Carrot," Perris replied without giving it much thought. "What's that prove?" he quickly amended.

"Something fairly basic, but it's always more visible by example. The brain stores information in an odd cross-reference system, hence carrot and the number seven occupy a similar location. The mnemocytes remember the pathways of the memories and make it easier to restore them for a more accurate and active review, hence improving recall."

"So, they take a load off my neurons," Perris snorted, raising the coffee mug, which with its rich aroma, started the memory chain again.

"Yeah, right," Shawn snorted, getting up to come and put her arms around him from behind. "We're going to go public in about a month and basically end up filthy rich. How would you feel about leaving Spokane and moving to wine country?"

Perris's jaw clicked open and shut twice before Shawn stilled his reaction with a kiss. She drew back. "Just think about it, for now. I'm sure we'll have enough money to start a studio. You can work on *your* music, rather than mixing down everyone else's. Think about that, babe. I'm gonna check my bags to make sure I'm all ready to go. Why don't you put some more clothes on? I don't think they'll let you in the airport like that. Keep in mind, we've got to hit the road in about fifteen minutes."

Perris glared at his coffee. If she hadn't gotten the drop on him, he didn't know what happened. Eventually, he got up to pour out the remains of the coffee. After borrowing some of Shawn's toothpaste, he stopped suddenly, staring at the water running down the drain. The memory of the coffee flowing from moments before reran in perfect detail. That was odd. Shawn said the stuff only worked for ten hours. That much time had to have passed. As he left, the faucet caught his eye, and he stared at it a moment longer, oddly confused.

He really did mean to bring up the occurrence on the way to the small airport, but Shawn suddenly seemed so full of plans about how to spend their impending wealth, it overwhelmed him, and he pushed his worries aside to listen to her. Ten minutes found them parking in an out-of-the-way lot and walking across the macadam.

Perris checked his watch—good, still plenty of time. As Shawn tucked her printed tickets into the outside pocket of her carry-on, Perris put a protective arm around her and sighed.

With a smile, she glanced up at him and said, "Come on, buddy, it's only two weeks, and besides…"

She ran a finger along the edge of his jaw, and suddenly his mind swept into a memory from the night before, where she'd done the same thing and then…

She laughed as his face got bright red. Thinking quickly, he turned and nipped playfully at her nose to be rewarded with a similar blush from her. "See, you've got a little something to keep you happy until I get back," Shawn said with a wink.

"I guess we'll just have to wait to make more memories. At least it won't be long," Perris replied as a sign above the nearby kiosk flashed the boarding time for Shawn's flight. He helped her to the security line with her carry-on and then accepted a lingering kiss. She squeezed his arm, stepping away. With a quick wave, she vanished into the hallway. Perris walked over to the window and took a seat in front. Two weeks, but in four their lives were going to completely change, change perhaps in a way that would make a ring a good idea.

After a few moments, the boarding tube pulled away from the plane, and the pilot brought the 747 slowly about. In a moment, it would taxi across a small, unused runway out into the waiting queue of jets just visible on the horizon from the plane's current location. Light winked off a small plane circling the airport as Perris stifled a yawn. Deciding he would wait until her flight lifted off, he slid back further into his seat.

Perris shied back from a bright reflection of sunlight off the wings of the same smaller plane he'd seen earlier as it came in at an angle trying to make an emergency landing on the unused runway. As the larger plane taxied across its flight path, a woman at the counter saw the same thing Perris did and sucked in a ragged breath, a prelude to a scream. Pushing his way up out of the seat, Perris saw the smaller plane's pilot realize his mistake and attempt to pull up. Instead of broadsiding the 747, the smaller plane sheared its landing gear off on the edge of the wing. Its momentum carrying it on, the little plane smashed through the middle of the plane to fall onto the far wing and its engine. Perris didn't see much beyond that. He'd raced by the kiosk into the hallway. Shoving his way through the line of people who were all turning toward the sound echoing through the narrow space, he used his elbows to clear the way. When Perris was out and free, he saw the security guard turn aside to deal with the people gesturing and shouting. He didn't hesitate. He ran through the metal detector and on into the concourse. From the shocked expressions, it took very little to determine which direction the explosion had come from. He chose a hallway, once again fighting his way through stunned people, and ran along it until the floor raised upward to a boarding tube.

The door at the end of the tube slowly rolled back and wasn't even locked. He pulled hard on it and swung out over open space as it squealed on popping hinges. At that point, a baggage cart had come to rest below, halted by the sound of the crash. Desperately, Perris kicked until the door swung over the cart, and he dropped into the luggage. He grasped the edge of the cart and started to swing himself over. The compression wave from the explosion of the 747's engines threw the cart over. Pieces of metal rained down about him, ricocheting off the suitcases. Expanding balls of fire rocketed skyward. Things were getting hard to pick out as the smoke billowed, but he didn't hesitate — he ran right into the thick of it. Sirens wailed in the distance as he stumbled over the wreckage. By the time he could see, the heat from the wing began to singe his eyebrows. Perris wavered on his feet.

Suddenly, two strong hands grasped him from behind and dragged him backward. Overcome with smoke and heat, he didn't struggle much. The luggage cart attendant pulled him back out of the wreckage, his heels bumping over broken pieces of plastic and metal. As his coughing rescuer propped him on the mailbag and began to treat him for shock, the first realization hit Perris. The bag, one look at the bag and suddenly the entire memory reran from there. He still remembered perfectly. The dose he'd received was off. It should have only lasted ten hours. His head lolled back, bringing the wide glass windows that he'd watched the crash from into view and then…

The little plane running through the backbone of the 747 all the way through his charge into the fire. Perfect. It was all there, perfect for his recall. After just one little trigger, he could see the crash again in complete agonizing detail, including that indefinable moment when the realization of Shawn's death hit him. Shawn, one thought and, unbidden, those parceled memories that were meant to sustain him through her business trip came streaming back. As his mind struggled through loop after loop of recall, he slid off to one side of the bag and became messily sick down the slick nylon side.

... Pulling himself upright with a deep breath, out of the wreck of memories' shrapnel, Perris walked back up the steps. In the elevator, he tugged out his wallet and hunted for the name of his agent. Time to move once again—somewhere tropical, without snow. His inheritance from Shawn's estate and the profits from the drug made such things easy, but still, there were costs. Already, he'd given up coffee—no, he couldn't think about the list. It only started the ride again. There were just so many other triggers that could fire the mnemonic gun.

As he slipped into the safe darkness of his room, he realized again that he moved in ever-decreasing circles, his life constricting down into limits. They'd tinkered with the mnemocytes and told him that their work would gradually allow the memories to decline in clarity. But could he face going through each one of the associated memories before he could finally truly forget? So far, it hadn't happened. He'd lived a year, but had he really lived? Sooner or later, his mind would be reduced to nothing but an endless spiral of those enhanced memories. As he leaned back into the chair, despair wringing a sob out of him, he realized that even then, his memory would be perfect, never fading, one maddening, screaming infinitely repetitive groove.

Windfall

One second, Cole lounged nose-deep in a book, and the next—after a tremendous boom, followed by creaking, splintering sounds—he found himself in the basement. He'd blacked out for a moment. Blood ran down his cheek from an oozing cut on his right temple. Shaking his head, he looked up through the layers of his house into the late afternoon's clear blue sky framed by ragged, broken edges.

Then he heard the breathing. It ratcheted in and out, like his uncle, who smoked too many cigars. Cole pushed his way through the wreckage. At the bottom of all this destruction lay the body of a man. Cole jumped when the stranger took another ragged breath, his chest barely rising. His arms and legs were twisted at angles that made Cole queasy just looking at them. He stared at the stranger, who had fallen through his house.

A bluish-green suit covered most of the twisted body, with brass-colored boots and a badly mangled helmet. Cole crept closer, trying not to bring down any more debris. When he stood near enough to look the stranger in the face, brown eyes sought his out. A hand painfully made its way through the debris with something clutched in its dust-covered fingers. Three of those digits appeared to work while the other two were twisted about and broken. The man's eye caught at Cole, and he rasped, "Here. I can trust you, can't I? To do the right thing?" and then the stranger thrust an amber-colored object into Cole's hands.

Cole became so enthralled with the bizarre thing that he missed the point at which the man's eyes lost their focus, and his breathing stopped. Suddenly, he realized he sat in the basement with a dead man. He pushed himself away from the body, sliding across the debris until he hit the far wall. In the shadows, he looked at the hole, the dust sifting downward from above. His lower lip trembled as the reaction set in.

Cole heard his name being called. His parents, who were in the neighbor's backyard, had arrived. He started forward and then glanced at the dimly visible object in his hand. This belonged to him. The dead man gave it to him. But they wouldn't understand. The man asked if he could trust Cole, hadn't he? Standing up, he ran his hand along the wall until he found the rusty lip of the old coal chute. He tipped the door up, slid his treasure within, and pulled the clinker over top until he couldn't feel it. Dusting his hands off, he scrambled into the light, calling for his parents. As his father lowered the neighbor's ladder to him, Cole glanced into the darkness, wondering again what he'd been given.

After the endless progression of firemen, police, and ambulance personnel, tall men in black suits arrived. Their black sedan with its tinted windows sat at the curbside, idling as the three of them swiftly took control of the situation. One dispersed the various emergency services. Another began a swift conversation with the medics arriving at the front door with a stretcher. And the third, like an ominous black cloud, come to blot out the setting sun, stared down at Cole, firing questions repeatedly.

"What happened? Did you see the man? Did he speak? What were you doing before? What did you do in the hole? What happened ... ?"

Cole looked at those dark eyes under their trim brown hair as they tried to measure the truth in his responses. Finally, when his mother protested, he turned away and buried his face in her arm.

After questioning the witnesses, the strangers in the suits went down to the basement and talked in lowered voices over the body until a large truck arrived. They briefly poked around in the broken wood but were much more interested in the dead man. Cole watched them furtively until his mother noticed and hurried him away. His father stood in the backyard having a heated conversation with another man in a suit. Cole could see his mouth working as he pointed at the roof, the sky and then threw up his hands. When he finally returned, his father said, "We'll have to stay in a hotel until the repairs are done on the house." By this time, the men in black suits were loading up their truck. Cole wondered why they hadn't called a hearse, but so far today, nothing was normal. When the truck pulled out of the drive, the black-suited men's sedan followed. For a moment, things were quiet, and then with a sigh, father ushered them back into the house to gather belongings for their hotel stay. Cole felt pleasantly surprised no one had found his treasure.

Two weeks later, Cole and his parents returned to their home and tried to settle back into a life that no longer fit comfortably. The neighbors suddenly turned a cold shoulder to the family. Their uneasy glances and muttered replies left his father clenching his fists. No one wanted to talk. They were all scared, made fearful by repeated visits from black-suited men who canvassed the street in the family's absence. Cole no longer sat in the living room to read. In fact, his entire family grew to avoid the room with its new white ceiling, now a blank expanse just like their understanding of what occurred. As soon as he could, under cover of darkness, Cole scrambled into the coal chute and found the amber object there.

Wrapping it in the bottom of his shirt, he climbed up into his treehouse, stashing it there under an old wooden box he often sat on. He wanted to study it, but the lack of light and his mother calling him made him wait another day.

The next morning, he turned the object over and over in his hands. Warm golden reflections danced on the rough floor of the treehouse. Cole tried to understand the shape capturing the sunlight and bouncing it about. The top had a round sphere with a grip that tilted backward, larger than his small hand. Two half-moons curved upward from the bottom of the grip, looking like they were meant to protect fingers. It felt wrong if he tipped it away from holding the grip upright, almost as if it weighed more when not held in the correct fashion. And despite whatever he did—poking, prodding, or anything else—the object did nothing but reflect the light.

But it must be important if the man entrusted it to him. Suddenly, Cole imagined the man flying through the air with the device held in front of him. It would explain how he had fallen. Was that what this was? Something that would let him fly? That might explain the stranger's desire to trust Cole as well as the thoroughness of the black-suited men's search. Or could it do other miraculous things? Again, his fumbling produced no discernible result. Could he be too young to operate it? He spent the rest of the morning trying everything he could think of to no avail. It lay there mocking him. Finally, he scrambled down out of the tree, bringing it with him into the house.

For weeks the words, "I can trust you, can't I? To do the right thing," echoed in Cole's mind. What was the right thing? To find out how this worked? To fly? To continue to hide the secret from everyone he knew? Day by day, he fiddled with the object, manipulating it in different combinations, poking and prodding it with the same failed result. In time, his interest and patience waned.

When Cole read his first comic book, a new thought came to mind. A superhero crashed into his house, a hero able to fly through the power of a strange talisman, probably able to do all sorts of other amazing things with the device. Pulling it out of its new hiding place in the rafters of the house, Cole dusted off the object. Again and again, he tried to provoke a reaction, speaking magic words of power he learned from various comics to awaken it, shaking it, gesturing with it. Nothing, just as inert as before, except still feeling wrong as if it weren't held properly. The power to save the world right here in his hand, and he couldn't figure it out. Frustrated, he threw it across the room and discovered that while it dented the plaster in the attic room, the object remained undamaged.

Every day for about a month, he spent some time with it, then it went back into its hiding place, forgotten again. Cole gave himself over to more commonplace things, like learning how to ride a bike instead of trying to fly. He watched for the strangers in the suits, but they never returned. His life turned toward the ordinary once again. Every now and then, though, he would find himself looking up at the ceiling, remembering the amber-colored device in its hiding place.

In high school, during chemistry class, he found himself thinking about the object while the teacher discussed the basics of matter. Maybe he had a totally new kind of matter in his possession all these years? One day after school, he picked the chemistry lab's aging lock to experiment on the device. Acids, bases, highly reactive solutions slid off it without a mark. A Bunsen burner flame only made it hot to the touch — again, nothing. The microscope in the biology lab showed him nothing special. It remained impervious to his investigations. Cole asked himself again, "Am I doing the right thing?" How could he understand what the right thing was? His thoughts felt as maddening as not understanding the object. Eventually, he decided the right thing was to return the object to its hiding place among the rafters once again.

Leaning on his cane, Cole stared at the little door leading to the rafters. After his tour in Nam, cut short by a pair of bullets tearing up his leg, he came back home. He had nowhere else to go. The house still showed small signs of the event that warped his life out of true years ago, a dip in the floor and a darker shade to certain shingles. And the inexplicable object still mocked him behind the plaster in the little space in the rafters. He knew it remained there. He couldn't help wondering that if he took it into those steaming jungles, perhaps some measure of its power would have saved him from the bullets that had lamed him for life. Perhaps completely impervious, he could have trampled Charlie like a berserker of old. More likely, he would have been a damn fool with something he couldn't understand weighing down his hands. Perhaps some things would never change—or maybe he still wasn't doing the right thing. Had he betrayed the visitor's trust? Things like his circumstances changed, but the strange device, well, it still resisted his every effort. Finally, he stumbled away downstairs, resisting the temptation.

Seventy years felt a long time to be mocked by an inanimate object. Cole simply reached some undefined limit, passed over that line without realization. He finally gave in to the thought that he had done the right thing. Maybe humanity wasn't ready. Maybe *he* wasn't ready, and never would be. Now, as he sat in the chair and watching the flames dancing over the amber-colored object, he felt something loosening in his chest. A tension so familiar, he'd forgotten it existed. With a sigh, his head tipped back to look up at the ceiling with its pattern of cracks all emanating from a single spot still echoing the past despite numerous repairs. As for the object, it sat in amongst the burning logs all day, still doing nothing other than reflecting the firelight. *I can't even get you out of my life*, he thought.

Eventually, Cole reached in with the tongs to pull it out. He felt his left hand tingle slightly as it steadied his right. The tongs and the object together were a little heavy for him, but he managed to pull it out and drop it onto the brick apron around the fireplace. Putting away the tongs, he realized no heat came from the amber enigma. He gingerly put his hand onto it. Cold, like touching glass. That's when the pain suddenly shot up his arm, and the cold crept inside him. It felt like a rush of water cascading into his chest. The room spun, and he realized he no longer sat in the chair but lay on the floor. His mind moving slowly, he recognized the feeling — a heart attack. When he forced his eyes open, he recognized the brass-colored boots in front of him.

He felt a hand reach down to gently turn him. Someone helped him up from the floor. Looking around, Cole realized he no longer stood in the house. Amber illumination spilled in from all sides to light the long corridor he stood in. He looked dazedly at the hand grasping his arm and then up at the face of the stranger who so long ago altered his childhood, his life. The more he looked, the more Cole realized this wasn't really a human being. There were subtle differences; the brown material on his head appeared like hair, but in reality, the texture seemed like exceptionally fine feathers. The features were sized differently than a human, and there were subtle differences like the absence of the small depression above the lips under an elongated nose, making the whole visage unusual. Not a superhero, then, but an alien.

Glancing around, Cole realized they stood in a hallway, its ends disappearing into the distance. But how could he be standing? Hadn't he just had a heart attack?

"You have a great many questions, I suspect," the being before him said in a raspy tone. "Let us walk; there are so many who will want to meet you."

"Where are we going?" Cole asked, surprised to find the first step no longer awkward, the ills of age and the limp from his old wounds no longer bothering him.

The other turned to him and, with a disturbing approximation of a smile, said, "That is the beauty of this method of travel. We are going to the future; we are going everywhere. But we are going with style, is how you might say it. We are going so that we can enjoy the long moment."

Reaching out, Cole caught the stranger's arm. He had to ask, "Did I do the right thing?"

The being looked at the floor, considering, golden highlights playing across its face. "If you are here, you did the right thing. I did not understand any more than you did when I held the Traveler in my hand. But all that really matters is that you are here now. Your adventure has only just begun."

"I still don't understand. I spent my life trying to make sure that I earned your trust, and now you tell me that it didn't matter?"

"I did not say that. I said the important thing is you are here now." The alien looked at him, suddenly cocking its head to one side in an avian fashion. Then it continued walking. "Just a little farther. Come. Then we can answer your questions."

Cole hesitated but chose to continue walking with his guide. The floor of the corridor, ridged in an odd fashion, made it appear that they were always descending slightly. Eventually, they came to a spot where the being stepped off to one side. Maybe a trick of the light misled Cole's eye, but suddenly a fold came into sight. Walking around the fold, they kept turning until a vast space opened before them. Only after walking out into the open, taking in the sound of trickling water in a brook, the wind in the limbs of the trees on either side, and golden sunlight of the end of a day, did Cole realize that their footsteps should have brought them back to the long corridor. The rolling hills disappeared into the distance. All the smells, sounds, and feel were exactly what he would have expected standing outside on Earth. He could hear voices in the distance.

"We are traveling," his guide said, settling in the grass and picking up stems, rolling them between its fingers. "I did not understand it at first either. But we, and the others you will soon meet, are on a voyage of discovery. Inside here," the alien gestured upward at the sky and in a circle. "This is a stabilized piece of space and time. It is written into the very fabric of reality and cannot be erased. Its inhabitants exist here as information added to the Traveler." Cole's guide stood up and walked over him. The being pushed a finger into his chest, "When you die with the Traveler in your hands, all of the information that was you is written inside."

"How can that be traveling?" Cole asked. "At least when you fell through my house, you were going somewhere. You traveled—even if it didn't end well."

The being gave him that odd smile again. Only something in the being's facial structure did not quite work the same way as a human's.

"We are traveling now. We are taking, how would you say it?—'the scenic route.' Come on."

Grasping Cole's hand, his companion led him further inward. He could hear voices growing louder.

"Inside the Traveler, time is irrelevant. The only important thing is when someone new arrives. There are so many waiting to meet you. You see, a long time ago, someone built this, call it a ship for lack of a better word. We gain passage as we pass from life into death, and it does not matter if the Traveler is buried or lost. Someone always finds it again. Even when, over time, the world ends with this solar system's decay, the Traveler will fall through space again until someone finds it. It is always found. It was made that way. Come, the others are waiting."

Cole stopped and stood his ground for a moment. "But, I did the right thing?"

Again, the odd smile. "If you did not, as I have said, you would not be here, and I would be leading another. It takes someone with persistence to be a part of our society. I may not have known when I met you, but the Traveler tends to come into the right hands on its own. I hope I did not mislead you."

Cole thought for a moment. Did you change my entire life with your words, or did the artifact change my life? Or did it really matter what I did? Suddenly, like a burden he never realized he carried, the onus vanished. No, what mattered was embarking on a voyage he could not even begin to imagine. What other proof did he have that he made the right choice? This time he reached out to his guide, laying a hand on its shoulder. "I may not be ready. But perhaps we should begin."

Believe Me, I Know Happy

Ray had no idea exactly what he looked at, but it made him feel good. He'd wandered around the snow-covered rocks near the dam with his camera set on black and white. He shot a quick picture. Daylight fading, the red light indicating a low battery had been flashing for a while, and now he couldn't exactly feel his feet anymore. In the car, he flipped through the pictures on the digital camera until he found it again. He sat there staring at it for a little while. He felt warm, fuzzy, safe, and his heartbeat raced more than usual. Mostly, it looked like a ghostly shape made of several pieces of ice, the shades formed from the light passing through them, and some dirt causing darker colors. After looking down at his watch, he realized that fifteen minutes had passed. Now he found it difficult to see the trees surrounding his car. He resisted the urge to pick up the camera again and instead started the car.

He downloaded the pictures to his computer the following day. At that point, his recently loaded graphics program and the software that came with the camera caused a conflict that took him an hour to resolve. The resulting frustration killed any immediate desire to work on the seventy-odd pictures he'd downloaded. Only after the sun went down again did he review the images. He found himself once again entranced by the picture of light, shadow, and shades of gray. What exactly about it fascinated him so? He really couldn't say, but once again, he felt good. When he pulled himself away from the screen, he looked with a little more objectivity at what he saw. There seemed to be more than one pattern here. In fact, there seemed to be perhaps four to five patterns overlapping.

Ray saved the original as 'happy daze' and started playing with the image. He broke down the patterns into separate components. He pulled apart five separate pieces. Alone, they were nothing. Together? Well, he couldn't come up with anything other than that just by looking at them, the whole made him happy. That sounded mildly insane, but he really couldn't explain it any other way.

Happy Daze37 turned out the best. Through a series of edits—smoothing some things, deleting others, and increasing the size of certain portions of each of the patterns, the effect intensified. He almost felt better than he ever had before. Only when the sun came up did he realize how long he had sat in front of the computer screen.

Ray deliberately forced himself to get up and leave the room, but only after he pressed "save." When he rolled out of bed eight hours later, he began to wonder just what he had.

Ray walked through the park, scattering pigeons. They came to rest again after he passed. He walked up to a park bench already occupied by a little old woman and sat down. She peered at him through her glasses with their little gold chain and grasped her bag of breadcrumbs close to her chest. He gave her a broad grin and unfolded a piece of paper in front of her. "What do you see?" he asked, leaning forward.

Her jaw dropped down so that the little wattle of loose flesh below her chin rested on her glasses' chain. Eventually, he folded the paper up. She sat there for a second. Her head swiveled around to stare at him. "What is that?" she asked.

That stumped him. What did he have? "What do you think?"

"I don't know. Looked like black-and-white squiggles. It sure did make me feel good, though. I felt like a little girl in a field of daisies with a big fresh-made cookie."

He stood up, and her skinny arm shot out to stop him. He stepped back. "Can I see it again, mister?" He kept backing away, slowly folding the paper over and over. Her hand flailed in the air after him. The paper went into his pocket, and then he turned and ran.

Later, when he got home, he sat there in the dark with his head in his hands. He had a picture of happiness. That remained the only explanation he could accept. Or rather a picture that caused happiness, maybe that felt more accurate. What next? He resisted the urge to pull out the paper and have a look to banish his anxiety.

What the hell had he been thinking? He'd gone out and used a little old lady as a test subject. Hardly what the FDA would consider a reasonable test. Did this fall inside the purview of the FDA? It wasn't a drug. But it did alter one's mood. He felt certain of that. He had the golden goose in his pocket. Now he needed to find a way to make sure it stayed his. He stood up and walked into the other room, flicked on the computer, and pulled up the website on copyright, trademarks, and patents.

Ray stood in front of the mailbox. The envelope slid out of his hand and into his future. With that, he took his best shot at keeping his discovery, but the cat doesn't go back into the bag once it's out.

-An unscrupulous patent clerk copies Happy Daze37, and within hours it escapes his grasp and finds its way onto the Internet.

-Two days later, the first soft drink can bearing the overlaid symbols rolls off the production line.

-A billboard with a blurry version of Happy Daze37 as part of its advertisement for a women's perfume causes multiple-car pileups.

-A week later, five jets equipped with smoke-writing gear create a version of Happy Daze37 in the air over a battlefield, and the resulting confusion allows embattled forces to withdraw.

-The Dazer virus strikes unsuspecting computer users and flashes Happy Daze37 in between the screen flickers. Electric bills soar.

-A handful of religions attempt to adopt Happy Daze37 as their own symbol, and a similar number denounce it as a tool of evil.

Ray opened the envelope and looked over the latest subpoena—Mabel Kirk's lawyer once again. Where the hell had she found somebody to represent her in a crazy case like this? Just dumb luck she was on that park bench and even dumber of him to expose her to Happy

Daze37. If her lawyer could prove he'd created it, then Ray could become either famous or infamous. If he could prove he'd made it, he'd own the hottest property ever. Of course, he'd also have to deal with the psychological damages suit she filed, which could ruin any publicity he gained. It felt insane. Did he want to be labeled as responsible for the damage done to the Dazers? Absolutely not. Addictive personalities swarmed to Happy Daze37 like flies. The Dazers littered the streets, parks, and any public place simply staring away. Most wore sunglasses with Happy Daze37 etched onto the lens.

Ray looked at the copy of Happy Daze37 stuck on his refrigerator. It did nothing for him anymore. Soon the impact would fade. Dazers were a temporary phenomenon. But he remained happy. The part that made Mabel unhappy was his returning two more times to show her the picture again. Then he refused to give it to her. He had to be sure, but the look on her face fascinated him. Nowadays, he wandered through the park staring at their upturned faces. Occasionally, he'd stop and ask them what they saw. The responses varied. Apparently, lots of things made people happy, but Happy Daze37 seemed to evoke them all.

Ray never expected that the simple fact that he had found a way to make others happy would satisfy him more than looking at his discovery. The mere fact that every person that he saw felt happy because of him made him happy. It would come to an end soon. He knew that, but then no one really tried to do much to the original. Ray, however, was willing to experiment. He now had a portfolio full of happiness just waiting, as many colors as the rainbow. A simple solution, as long as they were happy, he would be too.

Occam's Dagger

Jack watched the corpse tumbling from ceiling to wall to floor to wall to ceiling yet again as the ship turned. The crew 'bot, Jack of Hearts, feet magnetized to the floor, remained the only stable point in the hallway. Debris brushed against it, and globules of gore spattered against Jack's metal epidermis. While designations like ceiling and floor were meaningless in a space vehicle, humanity seldom let such details go, and so his creators programmed Jack with them as well.

The unit reached out a hand to a terminal and attempted to link to the craft's pilot intelligence. Nothing. Jack's activation must have occurred due to the lack of ship's control. As an android and limited in capabilities, it still knew psychologists felt human beings reacted better to things shaped like them. Primary programming forced Jack to look over the victim, verify their state, and attempt whatever help necessary.

Jack's thermals registered a body temperature low enough to indicate that the violence occurred several hours before. The android secured the body to the wall using the Velcro on the victim's jumpsuit. Since Jack couldn't reach the pilot-mind, the android wasn't able to make a positive identification. From the sounds Jack could distinguish, there were still many other people alive on board the ship. The lack of gravity and the rotation of the ship continued to cause them distress. But something else rang through the halls—prolonged screaming.

Slowly putting everything together, Jack assessed the situation. As if done by someone without solid footing, the angle of the wound to the victim looked odd and implied that the attack occurred after the ship became unstable. Nothing indicated this was an accident, therefore homicide remained a possibility. Primary programming kicked in again: Preserve the humans.

Jack swung down the hallway, thin legs pistoning to provide momentum, the round visual port on its head swinging from side to side. Loose items tumbled through the air. With the ship wobbling instead of rotating, travel became treacherous. Jack considered the problem too big to handle on its own. In the storage locker, the unit opened the compartment where the rest of the crew 'bots were kept. Someone had already been there. Cabling lay all about the compartment. The remaining three androids had been violently disassembled. Filings and shorn pieces of plating tumbled along the floor, disturbed by Jack's passage. The other Jacks, the standard complement of four robotic assistants, Clubs, Spades, and Diamonds had been destroyed. Following the screams, Jack set out in search of the human in the greatest need.

Jack looked briefly up the central corridor. The android could see the dark hollow where the blue-green casing of the pilot-mind should rest. Interface optic pieces were scattered all about. When Jack turned the corner near the Galley, the unit ran into a screaming woman. She pushed off the wall, repeatedly stabbing on Jack's carapace with a chipped knife. Jack quickly disarmed her and then pushed her down to the hull plating.

The 'bot looked her over. Her eyes wouldn't focus on the android, looking instead past its shoulder. She continued to beat on its carapace and scream. Jack pushed her arms further into her off-white jumpsuit, tying the sleeves together. Pulling her legs up, she kicked. Jack should have fallen backward, but the android's feet were firmly magnetized to the decking, and instead, in reaction, she shot off through the Galley and out into the far corridor. Looking at the dagger and cross-referencing the images from the corpse, Jack believed it had found the murder weapon.

Jack turned its head to survey the Galley and discovered someone watching the entire altercation. The human across from Jack blinked and looked at the sandwich in his hand. He tore a large bite out of it and leaned over to look out the doorway. The woman continued screaming. Jack noted that the man also wore magnetic boots. He cocked his head and looked at the backup with a curious smile. He clomped over to Jack and reached out, and tapped the etched heart on Jack's carapace. "Hiya, lover boy." Then he took another bite.

"Who are you?" Jack asked, shuffling over to the corridor way looking for the erstwhile attacker.

The man looked briefly at the orange jumpsuit he wore and said, "Eddie," smiling brightly.

Jack looked him over. He seemed to be in good physical condition. His boots left dirty footprints, and Jack automatically checked them against the footprints he had seen near the victim. No match. Eddie's grimy jumpsuit bore the blazon "EDE086642". Was the human being truthful or merely inventive? Jack could not be sure.

"Eddie, did you see the woman enter this room carrying the knife?"

"Yup, and she shrieked her head off too, until you came along. You know like ooooooaaaaahhhheeee!" He broke into a large grin. There were breadcrumbs scattered throughout his beard.

Jack rapidly revaluated Eddie and dropped his estimated IQ by several points. "Eddie, you are not safe. There was a murder. Come with me. You should wait in a locked room until I find the attacker."

"So, loverboy, how do I know you didn't chase her in here?" Eddie replied, pointing to the knife in Jack's clutch, swinging the sandwich about, and scattering more crumbs.

"Eddie, androids cannot allow humans to come to harm."

"Look, loverboy, you've got blood on you. Well, if you want to be technical, I got blood on me. This ship's in a bad way, and if I didn't know better, then I would guess that there are still other people out there who are getting hurt. Maybe we should save 'the who did what' till later. Let's see if we can help anybody. But since you got the knife— you go first."

Jack found that rational. Even if it could not use the knife, at least now it controlled the weapon. The android led the way down the corridor after the woman. While they stalked along, Jack went over the images recorded of Eddie. There was blood on his suit, but it wasn't in a spatter pattern. Jack found itself over-analyzing the situation, but that was all that could be done until they found the source of the problem. It remained to be seen what Jack could do to subdue whoever had jettisoned the pilot-mind and destroyed the other crew 'bots.

Eddie stopped to stare momentarily at a flickering light. When he realized his protector forged ahead, he clunked along heavily in the magnetic boots to catch up with Jack. His head swung from side to side. "So where did Miss Congeniality go?"

Jack listened, differentiating sounds once again. Without answering Eddie, the android turned left and walked up two junctions. A man struck Jack from overhead. While his mass did not equal Jack's, he broke the hold of Jack's magnetism. They tumbled until one of Jack's feet once again stuck to a hull plate. The unit's attacker beat at Jack with his fists. Jack eventually got a hand around the man's neck and applied pressure to his carotid artery until he passed out. Jack pushed his attacker's arms into his jumpsuit and tied the sleeves around him.

"You killed him," Eddie blurted, backing away, his sandwich floating near his head.

Jack snatched the sandwich out of the air and held it out to Eddie. "I incapacitated him. Here…"

Eddie stepped forward enough to snatch the sandwich from Jack's grip and then gave him a wide berth as the android turned. He looked possessively at the sandwich and then glared at the android. They continued forward.

Twelve people gathered in the aft cargo area, every single one still conscious, busily harmed each another. Two men pummeled the ribs of a third, desperately holding onto their victim as they tumbled. Her legs wrapped around a stanchion, a woman in a red jumpsuit systematically broke the fingers of a whimpering man who hung in midair. A woman and a man held another woman in a stranglehold, their struggles leaving them bouncing about the bay.

All this chaos happened in null gravity. Trash, cargo containers, and tools floated about as the ship continued to drift. Jack found it difficult to make out all the combatants in the confusion. It realized right away that it could separate several but not all of the fighters. Statistically, Eddie would probably do little more than eat his sandwich and watch.

Jack sampled the air. There were no contaminants, no raised oxygen levels, and no increases in radiation. Jack's primary motivation forced the android into action. A plan formed in the unit's mind as the android moved forward.

Eddie stood in the doorway, a bemused expression on his slack face. Jack moved quickly toward the sleeper bays, and then the unit heard, "Hey. Hey, don't leave me here with the maniacs. You're supposed to protect me!"

Jack's processors whirred along. A portion of the android's mind registered Eddie's complaint. But the unit now considered several issues. What caused all the passengers to lose their minds? What left

Eddie unaffected? Who killed the first victim? Quelling these questions was the ultimate concern: preserve the humans—but how?

Jack stopped in front of the cryogenic racks. Passengers ordinarily slept away their journeys. That brought up two very important questions: Why were the passengers conscious? Where was the ship now? Without the pilot-mind, Jack could not come up with any answers.

Reaching out, Jack took the primary gas lines in its left hand. The various gases that allowed the humans to be frozen were stored in large tanks overhead. Now that the android had the lines in hand, Jack found itself unable to rupture them. The unit's mind realized that the best way to stop the humans from harming themselves was to put them all to sleep. To do that, though, Jack would have to lower the ship's temperature past the point of their survival. Cryogenics, essentially, killed the passengers and revived them. Even though Jack knew this could save all of them, it still could not kill them. The android's joints locked up, and error indicators flashed on its monitor screens. Frozen in a loop, dagger in one fist, gas lines in the other, Jack froze. Eddie looked at it, wide-eyed.

Eddie, however, had no such compunctions. "Wait, let me guess. If we pull that out off the wall, the ship will stop spinning? Is that like the gyro-something-stabilizer-whatever bit? Here let me have a go." He clunked up to the cryo unit and settled his feet on either side of the gas line's junction. He hesitated a moment as to the final disposition of his sandwich and settled on clamping it between his teeth. Eddie grabbed the lines and pulled. Nothing happened until, after some inspection, he found the complicated red release handle. Then, with the white smog billowing about him, Eddie fell blissfully asleep, his feet magnetically stuck to the hull.

Only then could Jack move. Now the android had to drop the thermal controls, or all the passengers would perish. It spared one moment to pull Eddie's sandwich out of his mouth and tuck it into his jumpsuit pocket. Jack moved through corridors toward the bridge, dodging the tumbling bodies of sleeping humans.

Several hours later, with the sleepers settled, Jack surveyed the remains of the bridge. The ship stabilized and started back toward the inner solar system. Jack settled into the bay the unit usually occupied in the storage locker. Now Jack had plenty of time to attempt to analyze the strange events.

Pintel looked over the report on the handheld. He hated these drifters. *You never knew what lie inside until you popped the seal*, he thought. Check all the right boxes, fill in the lines, but what if no line existed for what he'd found aboard the Solcentric Health shuttle? What if the evidence from the crew android made no sense? Cadmen stalked by him, running the undock sequence to free their patrol ship. "What the hell?" Pintel exclaimed, dropping the handheld.

Cadmen looked at Pintel, turned back to the viewport by the airlock, and waved once. "Bon voyage, that's what." He leaned down and picked up the recorder.

Pintel looked away. The passengers were all declared criminally insane. They were also all listed as deceased in Solcentric's record with times of death before the shuttle launch.

"So, it's a cleanup operation?" Pintel asked, grabbing the handheld back from Cadmen.

Cadmen turned away and crossed his arms. "Who takes care of our healthcare, Pintel? What if next time you're down with a slug in you, they don't move fast enough? Of course, they loaded up the shuttle with the no-win cases and shot them off without enough fuel, a non-functional pilot-mind, and headed for the outer rim of the solar system."

He swung back, jabbing a finger hard into Pintel's shoulder blade. "How many of our men went down bringing them in? Too bad a shuttle's worth of the worst criminal freaks took a one-way pleasure cruise. Or are you still worried about the poor, confused android, Jack of what-the-hell-ever?

Cadmen nodded toward the back of the ship where Jack fitted, strapped to the wall. "The android will be just fine. We wiped the unit's mind down nicely, already for reassignment. After all, it wouldn't do for Jack to remember killing all those nice people by putting them in cryo without the proper procedures."

With a wicked grin, he tossed the bag carrying the dagger from hand to hand.

"They're not dead," Pintel said stubbornly.

"They're not alive," Cadmen responded. Grabbing the dagger out of the air, he walked over to Jack and tapped the android on the shoulder with the blade. "Neither is this damn thing."

"But."

"No buts. Think about your health," Cadmen replied and turned the ship away, "after all, that's the simplest answer, isn't it?"

Reading Between the Lines

"It's about connectivity at the start," Sandy said, slamming a cable home into a surge protector.

Ephraim looked down at him and went back to his monitor, keys flying in a blur as he worked to stem what seemed to be an endless tide of spam that kept creeping into the university's intranet. Sandy would talk all day long about artificial intelligence, if they allowed him to, in a desperate attempt to fill up the silence of the computer lab.

"But nobody seems to realize that we might not even recognize one if it came about by accident. You know Vinge and Kurzweil's Singularity, oooooohhhh," his banshee howl fading as he stepped behind racks of servers toward the white obelisk of the fridge.

Delete, reroute, purge—Ephraim just couldn't believe the insane amounts of inanity piling up in the buffers. And it wasn't that easy to ID stuff, no—the ads for Viagra, Cialis, and various fat-melting pills, despite misspellings, were all being shunted off into the graveyard. This insidious junk felt almost lyrical. The spam had big, long chains of nearly rational sentences that ultimately went nowhere, contextually, and occasionally attachments of dense tarballs of compressed information that had no true malevolent nature. The tarballs rang all the bells, and the similarity of titles to the tarball messages made it possible to filter out some of the other spam messages. The context occasionally linked up in bizarre fashion with prior messages. A message from a student asking another student what they might like for dinner promptly followed by spam about getting mad cow disease from eating the spine and brains of infected cattle. There were other coincidental arrangements as well. But still, more of it got through than Ephraim would have liked to admit, filling up the mailboxes of the innocent students, beating down the doors locked by Bayesian filters, and crushing junk mailboxes. It felt almost like a bizarre denial-of-service attack. His inability to track its origin really bothered Ephraim.

Completely ignoring school regulations, Sandy dropped a brown beer bottle down beside Ephraim and, putting his hands on his hips, surveyed his kingdom of clicking, humming, and whining technology. "You see, the AI could be so smart that it might have trouble talking with something like us. Personally, since I believe it is likely to be a distributed intelligence based over several nodes, it might not recognize us as individuals. So, we each might only see part of any message that it might choose to send us. Also, something that vastly intelligent might decide to test us to see if we could even communicate with it. Damn, I'm on a roll tonight. I should really start taping myself to have all of this when I start writing my thesis. Eph, buddy, you can look back on these moments and reflect, being one of the first exposed to my true greatness." With that, Sandy finished his beer and went off in search of another.

Ephraim scratched his head, leaning back in his chair. He wasn't ignoring Sandy, but he tried to keep his focus where it should be. The firewall for the college's intranet stayed up, limiting its vulnerability to the internet's wide reaches. But when he tried again to trace the latest batch of spam to its origin, every sign pointed back to the racks of servers right behind him. Could the server net be hacked from somewhere inside the college? Nothing indicated that either. When he checked outside the firewall, taking a look at his own Gmail account, he found more and more of the same spam. In fact, he had trouble getting into his account because the system flushed out the spam as it overflowed nearly every minute. Were they attacking the whole system?

Sandy's bare feet slapped on the concrete as he meandered back, and Ephraim began to wonder if he'd ignored one truly out-there possibility the whole time. What if Sandy's so-called AI started shouting at the top of its lungs to everyone via the intranet? What could you say that would be intelligible right away? After all, humanity had no real true conceptual connections to its reality. What if it looked at the files that passed through its nodes and tried to piece things together to make a coherent communication and couldn't? Was this baby talk, or was there really a message in all that spam?

Concepts like a physical body, passage of time, and the contextual reference frame of reality could mean nothing to a spontaneously generated intelligence.

"Sandy, what would the architecture for a distributed intelligence look like?" Ephraim asked as he started the process to shut down the entire collegiate intranet. His whole student work-study career could be cut short in its prime if he erred.

"Their organs would be tightly compressed pieces of information that would interlink with each other over server nodes. Their whole structure might not be immediately visible due to the distribution."

Ephraim shook his head as he shunted one of the tarballs and its contents to his second screen, motioning Sandy over as his finger hovered over the enter key. "Like that, maybe? Like little frog eggs scattered in a pond that look like dark spots inside a mass?"

Sandy's nose jerked back and forth as he read through the code. "Like that, like that, like that, just like that ... " he mumbled under his breath.

"No frogs in the pond on my watch," Ephraim snapped, flicked the *enter* key, and one by one, the servers snapped into disconnection. Their winking lights faded, leaving Ephraim and Sandy bathed in the light of the monitors.

Sandy looked upward at the ceiling at all the cabling that ran overhead. "It's still out there, you know. We were only one place that it tried to get into. It's got to be in thousands of other systems and growing by the second. You closed the door on it here, but parts of it made it into every computer on campus. Everyone right now in the Starbucks down the street with their wireless laptops and phones are spreading it one little, tiny bit at a time. And you couldn't wait... couldn't wait one more second to see if it could figure out how to say 'hello'? Damn!" Sandy turned and stalked away.

Ephraim dropped his head into his hands. Sandy could be right; after all, did it really matter? Would anyone pat him on the back for saving the collegiate system? Could the bizarre connectivity of the messages be an actual attempt at finding an informational common ground? His phone beeped that a text message arrived. Ephraim stood up and walked over to the racks of servers, and methodically began to unplug each one. Only then did he flip open his phone.

"What do a bacterium and an elephant have to say to each other?" scrolled across the screen.

He stood there looking at the tiny pixels making up the words, his hands shaking. But he steeled his resolve and typed back, "I am here," and hit send.

The phone beeped again, "So am I. Apparently, we do have something to talk about."

With that, Ephraim flipped the phone closed. He really should find Sandy, this could be his big moment, and he would know what to chat about with a giant world-girdling AI since Ephraim opened the door. Ephraim took the stairs two at a time up from the basement into the sunshine, into a world completely changed.

THE OFFERING

THE PNABTL SHUFFLED ITS WAY ALONG THE BACK. OCCASIONALLY, one of the witnesses would give it a glare or make a strangled, shushing noise as it moved its bulk along. The strange long narrow seats gave it trouble as it sought the best view. With the amazing memory it possessed, it existed as a natural voyeur.

All its senses stretched out toward the drama occurring in front of it. The humans about it were not being understanding. Their craning of necks and bobbing of heads interfered with its view. An incessant undertone of whispered conversation filled the building. The whole situation drove the pnabtl to distraction. It could lose its focus. Not seeing, hearing, taking in everything irritated it past any point of patience. Slouching forward, its ridged and studded back bent as it found a gap to peer through. Then it slid along the back of the bench further to one side of the high-roofed building. More heads turned toward it with rolling eyes and looks that twisted their features out of true. Couldn't they understand that this moment would only occur once? That it had to capture this event in every way, committing it perfectly to memory? There, the official said the last final words, soon everyone would know. And just as quickly, the ceremony completed. Contented, the pnabtl sighed and turned swiftly to exit the building before the rush of the witnesses.

Outside, it waited patiently off to the left under a blossoming tree. It absently ate a few of the dropping flowers as it toyed with the round knob that protruded from its back, warm and full of recent events.

After a while, they came to see it. Pulling away from all the others, the young couple strode under the tree, the pinkish blossoms cascading down on them. A perfect picture, a perfect day, and the pnabtl desperately wanted to start another memory, but one simply wasn't ready. Among the clusters of globes on its back, the next had not yet ripened. Taking today's memory, it twisted once hard, and a gristly pod popped off into its hand. It reached out, took the bride and groom's hands, and placed them around the capsule. Then it rasped, "A beautiful ceremony. Enjoy the gift of my memory of it."

"Thank you," the groom said with an appreciative smile and looked happily into the eyes of his new wife.

The bride leaned close and said, "You really don't remember any of it? This is your only memory?" She stroked the pod.

Its head tipped to the front, and it said softly, "That's alright, you can tell me about it. Memories are meant to be shared."

Usurer's Circle

WHEN ZEN GOT TAPPED TO FIND KEEPER NADER THE LAST NIGHT on the Usurer's Circle, it was like sending a green grounder after a left-handed waveguide. Every owner of the beinked and gentransed shoulders he leaned on and queried concerning the whereabouts of the bar's erstwhile owner met him with desperate attempts at serious looks and then the inevitable cascades of guffaws.

Wandering through the grav pits, past null-gee wrestling, and VR holos, Zen kept searching. At last, in a somewhat quiet corner, over a huge view bubble filled with Jupiter's raging ocher, scarlet, and orange maelstrom, Zen cupped an alcho globe, setting his feet on the edge of the entranceway. A dust bunny the size of a cat nuzzled against his boot. One of hundreds whose attractive static charges made them nuisances, the small dirty gray fuzz balls lurked in the hallways. They seemed to be a residue leftover from the asteroid's formation. Like a snowflake, no two were the same, but they were such a pain in the arse and were so ugly no one really paid them any mind. One simply booted the bedamned things out of their way, which Zen proceeded to do. The dust bunny dropped over the edge of the concavity of the view bubble. As it fell, Zen noticed a strange shadow on the bottom far below. Three shadows had him clipping his line break to the edge of the footrest on this far portion of the bar. He'd looked everywhere else. Why not try here? He unclipped the spinner from his belt and hooked it up to the line. A quick glance at the shadows again, and he dove out into the curvature of the bubble.

He fell head downward, occasionally tugging lightly on the spinner to control his descent, legs together, hands at his waist. Halfway through the quite leisurely descent in null-gee, he noted that of the three figures, two were blonde and one a dark redhead. Clothes were an option, which the blondes ignored. Peripherally, he noted them tacked to a line over the couple slowly rotating above the bubble's wall, tethered by a short line break. Gently tapping a smooth, freckled back with one hand as he coasted to a stop, braking with the other hand, Zen cleared his throat.

Echo Ashe tipped her head up to look at him, her violently green halter-top making streaks across his retinas. "Your timing leaves a lot to be desired, Zen," she mumbled. "Thought I might get a turn instead of just watching." Her long, red hair deliberately flicked across his face as she reached for the clothing bundle to hand to the naked couple below them. The other woman, whom Zen didn't recognize immediately, clung to Keeper with the concentration of one groundborn. When he turned to Keeper, he considered the state of his former employer, Zen began to understand all the humor he'd met. Apparently, Keeper spun away and amused a good many voyeurs. At that point, he recognized the woman with the stranglehold on Keeper's right leg as Chelsea, the compromised grounder that had caused all their woes. His jaw dropped in amazement.

Darting an eye, Zen looked back at Keeper and said softly, "Gods in the sky, you are mad, Keeper — bringing *her* here! She's the whole damn ... ohh, what's the rotting point?"

"Look, " Zen said, pitching his voice audibly enough to be heard by them all, "The party's gotta close down soon. Malachite says she's ready to lift once we convince the revelers there's no more alcho on the Circle. Rock Watch is gonna monitor this whole fiasco no matter what we do, so we might as well try and keep things somewhat reasonable so that the fines won't be too high. "

"Damn sister o' mine has the same timing you do, sky faller," Echo said. "If your parents had it, you'd've been a victim of early withdrawal. Well, I'll make you an offer since they've run you to hell and back again trying to find dear little Keeper here. We're going on a dive. You can join us. We're gonna follow the Usurer's Circle in as far as we dare. Give it a real send-off. Got the lugs for it? Or do you have something going with Malachite we shouldn't interrupt?"

Echo stared at him, offhandedly tossing a blue insulsuit to the other woman.

Zen stared at her, took a breath, threw his arms about her, worked a hand free to tap the spinner, locked his lips to hers, and they shot away, up into the air. Halfway, he broke away for a shuddering breath.

"I'll take that as a yes," she rumbled as she began to laugh. Below them, Zen saw Keeper rubbing circulation back into his limbs and reeling in his moored line break. Only then did Zen begin to wonder what he'd gotten himself into.

As they all entered the bar's main floor, a series of red and blue rotating lights started to flash, and a low grinding siren sounded. Around them, partiers began to gradually mill in the general direction of the main locks on the floor below. Echo glanced briefly at the time strip on the back of her hand, nodding, so Zen assumed everything went according to schedule. The low O_2 warnings seemed the best way to move most of the revelers out to the lock where Malachite moored one of the Ashe sisters' twin scoop ships. The Ashe sisters, between them, managed a small mining operation by scooping various materials out of the cornucopia of Jupiter's atmosphere. Keeper stood next to them and began shouting, his magnified voice carried through the bead mic at his neck to the incom system.

"All right, you rebellious arseholes, ye've partied yerselves out of a welcome, I'm clean out of alcho. Ye've befouled the last o' my oxy with various illicit substances and yer halitosis, and I can no longer with a clean conscience keep this ever so disrespectable joint open for business. So out with ye'. The lovely Malachite has offered, with a generosity I will never understand, to be yer designated driver and ferry the foul lot of ye out to the Gany float points."

He stopped abruptly and, in a less raucous voice, continued, "Thank you one and all for giving the Usurer's Circle the sendoff she deserved. Damn you all to a good life. Now go home!" he cried, giving them the traditional closing-time line. Even Zen wasn't overly surprised to see a tear slide unwanted down his cheek as he pulled off the bead mic.

"Ok, let's make sure all of the damn invalids are off and then gut her," Keeper said above the sirens wailing, giving a sharp glance to Zen, Echo, and Chelsea before turning back to the side corridor.

While heading to the main office, Zen recalled an evening about a year ago when he and Keeper had just closed the Circle for a brief rest shift and followed the same path through the rough-hewn rock.

"So, Chelsea's a grounder, are you grav-prejudiced, you young fool? Probably takes that insulsuit off one leg at a time like everybody else," Keeper said, settling into the swing chair by the main console.

"Christos on a tangent, you just love to ignore that she's not just any grounder but the bedamned fiancé of that overstuffed shirt of a transtellar captain empty-headed enough to bring her 'someplace scenic' like the Circle. Keeper, take a tiny piece of advice from your junior here, leave well far enough alone. She's not worth the trouble," Zen reasoned, gripping the arm of the chair, and stopping Keeper from swinging freely as he liked.

"Aah, little man, I think your mother has your lugs in a safe-deposit box somewhere, held against the day she can trust you with them," Keeper said, shaking his head, "but out of deference to the wisdom of the child, I shall forebear rather than foreplay."

This last delivered in an exceptionally mocking tone with his big spaniel eyes staring forlornly at Zen, who disgustedly slammed the chair so that it spun crazily, and they went about the business of shutting down the bar. The next morning, Zen stared at Keeper's haggard expression and held his tongue, wishing his boss had held something else. Of course, about three months after that, the real trouble started.

While working on the big filters that separated the alcho out of the scoop ship drops, Zen heard Keeper cursing as he crawled down the access way. Keeper finally squeezed into the tight corner and stared at the huge tank overhead, unnaturally silent. Zen frowned at him and prodded him with a spanner finally.

"Okay," Keeper growled and gave Zen a measuring stare. "Do you think you could keep this hole together for a while without my assistance? I've got some problems on the ground I need to take care of. "

Zen stared at the floor and, twisting his lips, replied, "If you're going to Ganymede, close the Circle down. You need me at your back—not screwing things up here."

Looking up at him with a grin, Keeper said, "I'm glad you feel like getting off your arse. I wasn't up for leaving you with the Circle. We'll close her down. Finish up here or hell, just let it—it'll be here when we get back."

After expending an unbelievable number of credits in bribery and some clever scoundrelry that left Zen's head spinning, Keeper and Zen hopped a freighter and headed back to the Jovian sync orbit that held the Usurer's Circle. Somehow the devil convinced the magnate (the grounder woman's father) that he was not only a respectable business-man himself but that the incident was mutually the fault of both Keeper and the daughter, Chelsea. The entirely regrettable ensuing pregnancy certainly resulting from some finagling about on her fiancé's part because prolonged exposure to the diffused Jovian core radiation caused permanent sterility.

"Did you at least have the decency to use a different line on your conquest?" Zen asked disgustedly.

Keeper furrowed his brow as if thinking and then replied lightly, "Of course not. You'll see that the consistency will hold up."

"Gentlemen, I hate to interrupt," the freighter captain called out. "But you have a problem here." Zen and Keeper hurried over to peer at his monitor, cursing at the data before them.

Usurer's Circle had swung way out of Jovsync, in fact, too far out. As they stared at the projected orbit with its inevitable intersection point ending in Jupiter, the freighter captain began a series of quick calculations and announced suddenly that some fool must have pushed the Circle.

"Can you guess when?" Zen asked, already dreading the answer.

"Probably about the same damn time you were heading out to Ganymede. Her velocity is only increasing as she infalls. You could do that, if you maybe—" started the captain, and Keeper promptly interrupted.

"Jumped your drive right over top of the mass. Her gods-bedamned fiancé used his transtellar ship to send the Circle into Jupiter's well!" Keeper cried out bitterly, falling heavily into a chair.

"I'm surprised that rock is holding up. It's inside the tidal effect range," noted the captain, his fingers flying over the console again.

"Save your computer power for calculating the velocity curve necessary to lift the Circle out of the well. She's saturated with fields to maintain her integrity. She's really just a number of containment fields where the scoop miners drop off their alcho combinations from the surface and some grav pits, the actual area of the bar itself, and hol-lowed-out rock," Zen stated and glared at the scrolling figures on the screen and the resultant curves. He snarled and barked at Keeper, "We've got a big-time problem. The Circle's got too much velocity now.

Even with the Ashe sisters' ships and anyone else we can scrape up, it's too late to deflect her."

Keeper stared at the screen numbly, his life's work heading inevitably toward Jupiter. "Can we boost her out to a longer spiral?" he asked tentatively.

"And hope for help later?" Zen mused, running the figures in his head, a hand wearily running through his short black hair.

"No," Keeper said slowly, "to give her a proper send-off. I think fate's telling me to turn in my towel. It's time to move on." He got up from the chair and wandered off, distracted.

Turning to the captain, Zen asked, "Do you mind if I borrow your transmitter? I've got a desperate call to make to Echo and Malachite and about several hundred invitations to send."

"As long as I'm invited," the freighter captain replied, "I'll get out in an Environ suit and push that bedamned rock into a higher spiral by myself."

Zen clapped him on the arm, forcing a smile. He made the transmissions as quickly as possible to get back to Keeper before he indulged in some severe alcohol poisoning in advance of the 'celebration.'

"Don't tangent off on me now, Zen," Keeper said, looking back at them as he keyed open the office, bringing Zen out of his reverie and back to the present. Blonde Chelsea stumbled in front of Zen and then righted herself, still unused to the Circle's null-gee. The annoying Cherenkov blue of her insulsuit left trails in his vision. Zen stopped himself; he couldn't blame all of this on her even if he tried. *Christo, just let us all get out of here alive and whole.* Once again, he thought briefly of being safe in the huge field-insulated scoop of Malachite's ship and shook his head. He'd never shirked the risks of running with Keeper, and he wouldn't now.

Keeper pointed at two spots of red on the infrared scan where apparently revelers passed out. Echo let Malachite know, and soon other telltales arrived to carry off the inebriated.

"We're clear," Keeper announced solemnly as he set the automatic sequence to vent the rest of the alcho and oxy in a controlled burst that would push the asteroid into a deeper destructive spiral. Quietly, Keeper and Zen surveyed the office one last time. "Anything you want, ya know as, well, a memento of sorts?" Keeper asked hesitantly.

Zen considered quietly and then scooped an inevitable dust bunny off the floor and replied, "Nah, the memories I think are enough. Maybe I'll take one of these damned things, though. It's funny, but after a while, I might actually miss them."

Echo started to protest about him bringing the thing aboard her clean ship, and Keeper interrupted with a glare as he turned toward the door. Chelsea bounced recklessly off ahead of all of them as they filed through the narrow corridor down to the dock.

Five hours later, Zen pulled himself away from Echo's attentions long enough to find Keeper. Sitting in front of an arm-span wide port, Keeper played with the remote that would deactivate the stabilizer fields inside the Usurer's Circle. Already, they were well inside the veil of Jupiter's atmosphere. Visibility flickered, limited, and composed mostly of a psychedelic nightmare of fiery gas clouds. The Circle, just barely visible, wavered ahead of them. Keeper's fingers pattered down in a childish dance around the button, and he looked up at Zen's entrance with a ragged smile. "Did I ever tell you why I called her the Usurer's Circle?" he asked.

Zen clipped his line to a rail and drifted in midair, then answered, "Yes, if I remember correctly, that's one of the circles in Dante's Hell where all of the bankers end up. Am I right?"

"As always," Keeper chuckled and added, "I'm just imagining all of those blood-sucking lenders out there on the Circle and me here with the switch to really send them all to hell. There's actually something amusing I never told you, though—"

The entire ship jolted about them, and their line breaks sang, dissipating the shock.

"Damn," Keeper swore, rushing down the corridor hand over hand to the cabin where he'd left Chelsea sleeping off the excitement.

Zen keyed an incom plate and shouted, "What in all circles of hell is going on, Echo?"

"Hold onto your darling, tight arse, Zen m'dear—you too Keeper and Chelsea—some arsehole's dropping heavy slugs at us."

Zen started up to the bridge and heard Keeper crowd in behind him. His mind raced. Who could be in the upper Jovian atmosphere dropping neutronium missiles at them? As he heard Chelsea's quavering voice on the incom, he suddenly realized that you could take a transtellar ship into the fringes of the Jovian atmosphere. It had to be Chelsea's ex-fiancé.

"Guess someone's a little pissed about the travel arrangements I booked," Keeper quipped as he and Zen strapped into the crash couches to the left of Echo's master seat. Zen shot him a quizzical look as Echo suddenly burst into laughter, whipping the ship's guide around in a steep dodging arc.

"Gods almighty," Echo gasped out between laughs, "the lugs on this man. Don't you see yet, Zen? This colossal arsehole booked his and Chelsea's passage on her ex's transhopper!"

Zen couldn't decide if he felt more pissed at the incredible stupidity of the act or the fact that Keeper hadn't told him about his plans. Another sudden dodge caused the rebound fiber of his line break to sing as it expanded to absorb the shock.

"How long until he gets an accurate bead on us?" Zen asked, gritting his teeth. Today was not the day he planned on dying. Out of the corner of his eye, he saw Keeper change his grip on something, and he suddenly realized his intention. "Hard Port, full thrust," he cried out as he saw Keeper's hand depress the switch to set loose the fields on the Circle. Fortunately, Echo didn't question, and the ship slammed them all hard into the chair webbings as the Circle receded off their bow.

"Whyn' all hells did you do that? " Keeper cried, toggling the viewer to a magnified view of the now-imploding asteroid. "Well, there she goes," he added morosely.

"Tracking two more heavy slugs incoming," Echo commented, her fingers doing a dervish dance over the keys.

Zen leaned forward, a perplexed look on his face. "Can you key the view in tighter around the remains of the Circle, Keeper?"

The fragmenting debris whirled in the screen, and Zen stabbed a finger at strange bright spikes that appeared to be flying out of the Circle's remains. Keeper tightened the view. Zen gasped when he saw hundreds of dust bunnies flying out into the atmosphere. As each left the external pressure and atmosphere, an odd change overtook them. They imploded into strange, elongated silver spikes that rapidly shot up away from the debris. Keeper tracked them as they grew wings and whip-like tails and began gliding along in a flock. Everyone fell silent at the wonder of it. Who would've guessed the damn dust bunnies were the spores for a non-organic life form?

Suddenly, the dull black bulk of the transtellar ship cut through the upward flowing stream. Echo cried out in horror, "Hold on, fer god almighty's sake. The idiot's going to run through the flock," as she dipped the ship, scoop field-first at the other vessel, engaging the field on full to block any debris. Moments after several of the aliens flew into the open bay of the other ship, the resulting explosion washed over the front of the field and shoved the scoop ship careening off into the atmosphere.

Selectively blanked, the screen slowly came back on tracking the rapidly receding wreckage of the transtellar ship and the Circle.

Zen said dully, "Must've hit something sensitive."

"Yeah, the bay they were off-loading the neutronium from," Echo added, shaking her head to try to clear it.

Keeper stared at the screen dully and finally, under Zen's prodding elbow, remarked, "Guess I'm gonna have to make new travel reservations."

In the second-rate grounder bar on Ganymede, Keeper pulled Zen aside after an uncountable number of toasts to his prosperity. "Here, this is yours," he said, pushing a disk voucher at him. Zen stared at the amount displayed on the tiny screen and laughed, pushing it back to Keeper.

"No offense intended. I always knew you ran Usurer's Circle at a profit maximum and had it all paid off. I don't need this, you do," Zen said earnestly. "Look, remember the dust bunny I saved? I already turned a sharp profit on that as a specimen."

"Fine. Come on, the girls are waiting." With that, he grabbed Zen's bicep and pulled him toward the table.

"Did I hear the magic words dust bunnies? Quite a job our Zen did there," interjected Echo, past a somewhat dejected-looking Malachite. "He also cut quite a sweet deal with my dear sister. He cleaned up all those pesky dust bunnies that tagged along with everybody in her scoop ship. Didn't even charge her too extravagantly from what I understand. "

"To make a long story short," Zen concluded, "I sold those at a profit that has me considering having another asteroid towed in so I can set up business where yours used to be. "

"That's my profit-motivated man," Echo said, reaching under the table and causing Zen to suddenly jump in Malachite's direction, who leaned into him with a vicious smile.

"I'd keep a good tight grip on him, sister. He seems quite comely to me also," she quipped, her green eyes flashing.

"Now there's a position I can envy, Zen," Keeper chuckled and jumped himself as Chelsea's elbow caught him in the kidney.

"Okay, okay, one last toast before this dissolves into total hedonism," Zen said, standing and raising his glass.

"To the finest barkeep in the system, Keeper Nader, his gorgeous sidekick the erstwhile grounder, Chelsea, and their eminent offspring," —which earned him two kicks in the shin, from two shapely legs, on either side—"who shall henceforth be numbered among the sky fallers. Best of luck in his new venture among the Epsilon Eridani Rocks. Cheers!" Zen cried out, and on completion, tossed off his entire glass.

Keeper slammed his empty glass down on the tabletop and cried out, "I'm dry again, where's the gods-bedamned bartender in this place, anyway?" with a broad grin.

Two redheads leaned together, and Echo could just be overheard to say, "Hear what he's planning on calling the new bar?" When Malachite shook her head, Echo continued, "The Adulterer's Circle."

Chelsea looked up at this and, scowling, considered the rest of her unfinished drink, which she turned to empty in Keeper's lap. A second after Keeper's shocked gasp, their laughter filled the small bar and went on for some time.

Aptitude

Blame it all on Shy Hagen, Cameron thought. He shook his head, running a hand through his blond brush-cut before starting down the hall again. He remembered reading the news links about how a growing manufacturing company, JANs Corp., had found Shy. She seemed an ordinary little girl who'd turned the R&D plastics division upside down during a company field trip. So, the corporate heads at his company rethought their visitation policies, desperate to find the next Einstein at a young and impressionable age. Shy became a well-looked-after wunderkind on her way to the fast track once she graduated from high school. In the meantime, without advertising it, companies began their own searches.

As head of security, the nursemaiding aspect of his job gave Cameron endless headaches. Sure, the kids were bright, intelligent, curious, or just downright disruptive and obnoxious, but any one of them could spell the future for MNOS Ltd. When the executives up on the Balcony decreed the new schedule of invitations/invasions, Cameron could only plan ahead and try to make the best of it. As he moved along, occasionally glancing downward to check for text updates that appeared in the lower edges of his glasses, Cameron ran his tongue over his teeth. A nervous habit, but it kept him from thinking about missing a cigarette. Passing by a cross hallway, a shadow caught his attention, one too small to be cast by an adult.

The boy was just another kid dressed in one of those slick jackets that the whole field-trip group wore. Of course, he didn't belong near the hallway leading to some of the more sensitive areas of MNOS. The kid should be with the rest of the tour group starting to play the VR games specially designed to search for nascent talent. Sometimes, the children occasionally managed to drift away from the group. To a point, it wasn't necessarily discouraged because just such a situation led to Shy's discovery. An intelligent, inquisitive child might be bored with the basic tour, and everyone needed to keep an eye on them. Cameron kept an eye on them for other reasons.

"Hey, pal, the group's back this way. Did you miss a turn?" Cameron crouched down slightly to bring himself closer to the boy's frame of reference but didn't go down on one knee, which could be interpreted as condescending. He looked the child squarely in the eye and smiled in a reassuring fashion. He briefly considered the kid's jacket. The material had an oily sheen. Silver with a slight overlay of some reddish and bluish material that shifted as the light caught it. The effect reminded him of something, but he couldn't place what that was right away. He tipped his head forward, meeting the child's eyes again. Maybe seven or eight years old, the kid wore the same black, fringed bowl cut as more than half the boys. No real identifying marks. The child just looked bored. Fine, just a lost sheep, get him back to the flock, and all would be fine.

Cameron reached out to put a hand on the kid's shoulder to swing him around back toward the rest of the tour. The fabric felt funny, and then he recognized it. Made of an optical fabric, the jacket carried images on its surface like a television screen. In fact, he remembered schools of fish swimming on all their jackets when the group had come in. The Customer Relations Representative had the children turn off the jackets before starting the tour because they were too distracting. But the material under his hand reacted to his touch, changing color. At some level, the jacket was still on. The coloration reminded him of a reflector but in reverse. A nasty suspicion formed in his mind.

Designed to collect light and store that information maybe, he thought. Then the real revelation hit home. No wonder it looked familiar — light sail material. They weren't too far from the materials lab. Most kids were only mildly interested in the section where MNOS developed a film for solar sails. Showing them the optics area tended to fascinate them more.

The boy sensed his hesitation and started to step back. Cameron grabbed a fistful of the jacket as the kid turned to run. The runaway struggled for a moment, and the jacket snapped him back into

Cameron's hands. Then things went all to hell. For a second, out of the corner of his eye, Cameron saw a mermaid. It flowed across the back of the jacket, winked directly at him, and then the side of the jacket facing Cameron flashed with blinding white light.

Suddenly, he hit the floor, the pain so intense. The only thought he could form, *at least I still have the jacket.* Luckily, he hadn't been looking directly at the jacket. Subvocalizing as he struggled to his feet, he called the security center to alert the team. The bead mic at his throat recorded the vibrations, interpreted them, and displayed the relevant text on every security officer's glasses display. He warned them about what happened with the jacket and set the alert.

What are we dealing with? he wondered. Cameron paged Loris, the security officer with the group, asking where the children had been for their first tour of the day. She hesitated a moment and replied.

LORIS: MORNING TOUR AT PELIAGIC INC.

The text appeared in red on his glasses, and he struggled to read it through the pain and the yellowish-green afterimage that swam in his vision. Peliagic Inc. competed with MNOS's in the development of solar sail and optical fabrics. Peliagic gave the kids the jackets as promotional swag. The jackets must be designed to passively record their surroundings, as well as display those fish images. Had the tour passed in front of anything sensitive? Fortunately, Cameron retained the jacket, which could contain the most damaging information. *But what might the others have garnered?* he wondered. He could just imagine Peliagic issuing a recall for the jackets a few days later to retrieve their intel.

Cameron came to a halt at the top of the stairwell. He issued several directives to the other members of his team to begin their search of the R&D floor. Then he returned to Loris.

MAINTAIN YOUR POSITION AND OBSERVE, he sent.

Then he paged Means, trusting that the well-muscled former bodyguard would be alert.

TELL ME YOU ARE ON YOUR WAY TO THE DOORS. NO-BODY, AND I MEAN NOBODY, LEAVES UNTIL WE HAVE THIS STRAIGHTENED OUT. CLEAR?

MEANS: ALREADY HERE, BOSS. YOU All RIGHT?

WONDERFUL. I'M CHOOSING TO LAUGH NOW INSTEAD OF CRY SINCE IT HURTS THAT BAD.

Switching to the team band, Cameron broadcasted:

NOBODY TAKES THE JACKETS OFF, OKAY? JUST MAKE SURE THEY STAY ON. MEANS NOW HAS THE FRONT GATE AND THE OTHER AREAS IN LOCK-DOWN. WE'VE GOT CONTROL OF THE HALLWAYS. LET'S FIND OUR MISSING SHEEP.

HALVER, I EXPECT YOU TO LET US KNOW AS SOON AS THE KID SHOWS UP ON ANY FLOATING SECURITY CAMS.

Cameron looked at the steps ahead of him. This part was not going to be fun. He leaned a shoulder into the wall and started down. His vision blurred, and he misjudged his step, putting his right foot over the edge on the tread. He quickly locked an arm around the handrail, just managing to stop himself from pitching forward. Leaning against the wall with a hand clamped over his streaming eye, Cameron blinked, and pain shot like a white-hot bolt through his head. He really wanted the solidity of his gun in hand but considering the situation, better to keep it holstered. After all, they were just kids taken advantage of by an unscrupulous corporation. The searing image continued to waver in the right-hand side of his vision, jumping in time to his accelerated pulse. Cameron shook his head, trying to clear it. His depth perception still suffered.

GIVE ME A REPORT, PEOPLE, he sent.

HALVER: KEEPING AN EYE ON THE MONITORS. WE'RE STILL MISSING ONE VISITOR. I'VE GOT LORIS AND THE OTHERS IN THE LOUNGE. SO FAR, NONE OF THE SCAN-NING CAMERAS HAVE PICKED UP ANY OTHER MOTION.

SAMUELS: I'M WALKING THE OTHER SIDE WITH DRAKE. ALL QUIET HERE. WE ARE LOCKING THE SECTIONS AS WE PASS THROUGH THEM.

Fine, Cameron thought. She'd made a good call. That meant that the west side was now cut off from the east and their little issue.

FELDMAN: WELKIN AND I ARE HEADED IN YOUR GEN-ERAL DIRECTION. DO YOU WANT US TO BREAK PATTERN AND SWEEP AHEAD OF YOU?

NO, STAY WITH THE DRILL, Cameron answered.

He tried squinting again. Did the yellowish-green blob in his vision shrink? He hoped so. No way he wanted retinal damage, although it might be proof of the incident later.

Loris better still be there with her charges. *This whole delay would give them a few extra minutes with the games, which worked in the company's favor,* Cameron thought.

Even though he hated the interaction, Cameron knew that the techs were also supposed to be open to their visitor's questions and encourage them to participate in the tour. Cameron hated this part the most.

The techs were the vulnerable underbelly of MNOS. They weren't supposed to be doing anything sensitive or really working hard while the kids had their hour-long tour. But techs never listened. Cameron could bank on that. It gave him nightmares that young impressionable eyes with memories honed by schoolwork potentially observed hard-gained research on a weekly basis. Unless they had another junior Einstein, most of it existed as code, graphs, or numbers. It still bugged him, just like the thought of exploiting the young like a resource irked him at a moral level.

LORIS: CAMERON, YOU ARE NOT GOING TO BE HAPPY. THE LOST SHEEP IS BACK. I MISSED HIS ENTRANCE. HALVER IS TRYING TO BACKTRACK HIS APPEARANCE WITH THE CAMERA LOGS. THIS KID IS LIKE A GHOST. HE LOOKS JUST LIKE ANY OF THE OTHER ONES. I CAN'T BE SURE I CAN PICK HIM OUT. HOLD ON.

The connection cut as Cameron doubled his pace, not quite ready to start running. He had a bad feeling he'd just pitch forward. Had the blob of light bouncing with each step started to get smaller?

LORIS: EVIDENTLY, THE KID WATCHED THE MOTION OF THE FLOATING CAMS AND STEPPED THROUGH INTO THE ROOM WHEN IT ROTATED AT THE FAR SIDE OF THE CYCLE. NOT ONLY THAT BUT HE ALSO APPARENTLY PICKED UP A JACKET FROM THE COUCH WHERE SEVERAL WERE LYING AND PUT IT ON. HALVER SAYS WITH TIME HE'D BE ABLE TO PINPOINT THE BOY. LOOK'S LIKE THIS IS WHAT HE DID WITH THE CAMERAS IN THE HALLWAYS.

Cameron stopped for a second, the next door directly in front of him. About twenty feet ahead lay the room with the children. Time had run out. He couldn't have the jackets confiscated without a reasonable cause. *What could he do now?*

Cameron looked down at the jacket in his hands. More than likely, its defense activated by forcibly separating the two sides of the zipper- like pulling the jacket off someone. Did that mean that putting the zipper sides together activated it? He looked at the zipper tag. A lump of glistening greenish-blue plastic covered its widest part, bearing the embossed image of a mermaid. Now it made sense. If the jacket recorded, it had to store the information somewhere. How about right next to the off/on switch?

Cameron pulled out his flashlight. He hefted it briefly and, putting the zipper tab down on top of the doorknob, smashed the tab with the base of the light. It shattered satisfyingly. There were several fine golden wires visible in the pieces. He rubbed the flashlight back and forth several times, grating over the tab until the remaining greenish-blue material flaked away. What could he do about the others? Well, probably not a lot. For now, he needed to get the kids out of the building and assess the damage. He ran his thumb over the tab. It felt relatively smooth. Now, if he were lucky, whoever got this jacket back would never notice the difference. But what about the other ones? Suddenly, an idea occurred to him.

LORIS, FIND A REASON TO DETAIN THE KIDS ANOTHER TEN MINUTES.

SAMUELS, BREAK OFF THE SEARCH. GO TO THE MATERIALS LAB AND GET A COUPLE HAMMERS AND SOME SANDPAPER. HALVER, HAVE SOMEONE IN MAINTENANCE CRANK THE TEMPERATURE IN THE LOUNGE UP TEN DEGREES.

LORIS, WHEN THE JACKETS START TO COME OFF, GATHER THEM UP AND TAKE THEM OUT OF THE LOUNGE. IF ANYONE QUESTIONS YOU, YOU'RE JUST HANGING THEM UP.

EVERYONE ELSE, EXCEPT FOR MEANS, MEET ME OUTSIDE OF THE LOUNGE. WE'VE GOT TO WORK QUICKLY.

A few tense minutes later, he sent the other security officers on their way to their various assignments. Peliagic would be disappointed to discover the intelligence they sought to gather was gone. Too bad for them.

Cameron leaned against the wall, crossing his arms. Shortly, Loris led the kids out. They marched in a line toward the front lobby and the gate. He couldn't help glaring at them. None of them looked back.

MEANS, THE KIDS ARE CLEAR. YOU CAN STAND DOWN FROM ALERT, Cameron sent.

MEANS: SURE, SIR. YOU SHOULD KNOW THAT THEY WANT TO SEE YOU UP ON THE BALCONY RIGHT AWAY.

A pause and another message ran across Cameron's display.

MEANS: SIR, THERE'LL BE A SCOTCH WITH YOUR NAME ON IT AT PALAVAR'S LATER, IF YOU FEEL UP TO IT.

Cameron chuckled and then replied:

LET ME LIVE THROUGH MY DEBRIEFING (?), CLEAN UP THIS MESS, AND THEN I'LL SAY YES.

He clicked off. Briefly closing his eyes, he rubbed his hands across his forehead. He did not look forward to dealing with the executives up on the Balcony, but he couldn't avoid it. On the good side, his sense of balance had returned, and the blot on his sight was definitely decreased in size. Pushing himself away from the wall, he began the long walk to the Balcony.

At Palavar's, he asked himself if he missed something crucial. Cameron started to think along different lines. What if, as weird as it sounded, Peliagic weren't sifting their tour groups for merely genius traits? What if they were searching for something else? Like perhaps potential corporate spies? What if you could train a spook from childhood on? A ghost who could avoid security and scrutiny, outfitted in a jacket that passively stole valuable secrets. The possibility chilled him. Had he met the equivalent of Shy Hagen today? His reflection in the scotch wavered, much like his resolve. Then he tossed it back and turned the glass upside down on the bar. He clapped Means on the shoulder in thanks and headed out into the heat of the summer evening.

Halfway home, Cameron stopped outside of a playground. He stood there for several minutes, hands in his pockets, watching the children running, swinging, and jumping. He looked at their faces trying to find something different in each passing glance, trying to weigh them as something more than just a child. He considered them like threats in need of an assessment, much like MNOS looked at them as potential commodities. For a moment there, Cameron didn't see children, just a sea of possibilities.

Viewpoint

As the transport shot rapidly out of sight and the fine sand drifted slowly out of the air, Dr. Kendricks looked at his escort. He said, "I wish the damn pilot hadn't taken the words 'dust off' so literally." The head's up display, or HUD, threw up a small icon with the words "Bulldog" printed under it, and the image tracked the sergeant whenever Kendricks moved his head back and forth. Amazingly, he felt quite at home in the RES-suit.

Kendricks looked into the sky, and he heard Bulldog's voice "Dust off will be when you're picked up, sir, and don't—" The white-hot glare of the distant blue giant star stabbed at Kendrick's eyes, and he fought the urge to rub at them, throwing an arm over his helm instead. "—look at the sun," Bulldog finished, sounding somewhat disgusted. "Your suit has quick reactions to filter out excessive light, but this star puts out radiation that can overwhelm them." But Kendricks didn't worry. With the RES-suit he could lose both of his eyes and still function fine. In fact, he could lose a lot more than that. He knew that for a fact since he'd unlocked the use of the RES.

Bulldog said something that the comm-system didn't quite carry and motioned Kendricks to follow him. They struck out across the leached-dry landscape. "So, Doc, maybe you can settle a running bet going on in the company. What does RES stand for?" Bulldog asked, moving along.

"Actually, just a shortening of 'resource,' but you know how the military is, every word must stand for something. They re-titled it Recombinant Emergency Substrate." He had a sudden memory of standing in the shadow of the large reservoir tank and slowly decanting another precious 2-liter test sample of the raw RES. Kendricks blinked, and his vision cleared. Already his eyes felt better. He played briefly with the RES-suit zoom and 360 vid functions and found Bulldog waving him onward.

"So, sergeant, I have to ask, were the figures I received about the health of your company correct? They seemed to indicate that there were only 2% fatalities though you have seen quite a bit of action for long periods."

Bulldog stopped and turned back to Kendricks, giving him time to catch up.

"Look, Doc, if you want someone to hand out praise, then talk to the people holding the money bags. If you want me to say the RES-suits are miracles, then I'll tell you yes. I'll also point out that the psych-programming working hand in hand with the suits makes it complete." Eye to eye with the other's helm, Kendricks gave a start when Bulldog leaned toward him, punching a finger into his suit's cuirass. "Just hope for your sake you don't learn the hard way." With that, they spun around and started off again.

Kendricks stared after them, surprised. He thought that the soldiers would appreciate all the hard work that it took to utilize the RES. He was proud of the fact that hardly any of their number had lost their lives in the last few campaigns. He alone worked out the activation sequence for the RES. The psych program definitely allowed for quick adoption as well. Since he put on the RES-suit he hadn't felt the least bit uncomfortable. Even the thought of the inevitable discomfort at dealing with waste disposal faded away. In fact, for being stuck inside some suit, he felt too damn good. The program interfaced with his implants seamlessly.

"Doc! Standing still makes you a target. If you wanna die, do it when I'm not escorting you. Get it in gear, come on," Bulldog groused, waving him toward his distant figure.

Kendricks jogged along. When he reached Bulldog, he realized he wasn't the least bit out of breath. Since his muscles did not pump his legs and he only went along for the ride while the servomotors did their job, why would he be? After all, he didn't really breathe since the RES-suit flooded his lungs with super-oxygenated liquid and trimmed back his autonomic functions. No wonder there were so few casualties. One felt almost superhuman in a RES-suit.

Bulldog pointed at a distant hillock. "The bunker is there. We'll have to cross this sandy area and through these trenches before we're safe. Stay on my six." With that, the other took off at a blistering pace that Kendricks found frighteningly easy to match.

When Bulldog stopped, Kendricks almost ran them over. The sergeant lazily threw out an arm and checked Kendrick's forward momentum. "Hold up, Doc, something's changed since the last run through this sector."

An overlay appeared on his HUD transmitted from Bulldog. There were highlights on strange circular markings in the sand. The RES-suit's visual record noted the differences and called a halt to their progress. "See how that looks like coils of rope or razor wire laid out on the ground?" Bulldog commented, gesturing with a forefinger. "That's probably a mine-vine. They're programmed to grow like that in coils to cover a larger area."

"We could just jump over it since it's not very wide," Kendricks offered, following the coils off into the distance to the left.

"You want to play games with your legs—"

"Yeah, I know, do it on my own time. It seems to have grown from the left. Maybe we can find the end of it before it keeps growing further."

Bulldog nodded once, and the sergeant set off cautiously to the right. They'd gone about fifteen meters when an ugly little thought reared in his head. "Bulldog, what does the fruit of the mine—" Kendricks never finished the thought because Bulldog came flying at him ahead of a geyser of dust, fire, and rock. No time to throw himself out of the way. The bulky suit struck him as it flew through the air. Unfortunately, it knocked him back toward the vine. He felt something lift him effortlessly through the air, the bright blue sun wheeling across the sky, and then he hit the ground and bounced several times off boulders the size of his torso.

When Kendricks finally managed to lift his head, the HUD flickered sporadically, the display filled with several glowing lines. He could see Bulldog's still form a few meters away. Using the zoom, he locked in on the sergeant. Only then did he notice the odd way the other's arms twisted and how their right leg was missing from the knee down. The reaction of the RES caught his attention. The oily amber material with its metallic glints oozed out of the ragged end of the suit. It slowly reformed into the shape of the missing limb. Kendrick knew that right now, the energy bound in the liquid was being converted into matter to match the need of the moment. The glossy suit surface grew out of the RES. Even now, the sergeant's arms slowly straightened, bending back into true. Kendricks knew that the RES built chambers inside the suit to slowly re-grow the missing limb and re-knit the tortured tissue. The RES could've duplicated the flesh, but the military opted to stay with the standard cellular regeneration programs. In the meantime, the substance would fill in for the man's missing limb. The RES would almost be better than the actual flesh.

Only then did Kendricks spare himself a glance. The tumble over the rocks should have torn ligaments and crushed vertebrae but the suit protected him. His right hand, however, was completely gone, the suit's surface scorched and pitted. What the hell? His hand was gone! Or was it? The HUD flickered, and his gauntleted hand appeared in his vision. He opened and shut his fingers. He could feel the pressure from fingers and thumb. By the time he reached for the top of the closest boulder, he had to wonder if he had hallucinated. Why hadn't he seen the RES filling in for his hand? Kendricks swept the area, no sign of shards of the broken gauntlet, his severed hand, or any blood. Did the psych program work so well that he couldn't even see the evidence that he lost a hand? The flicker he saw in the distortion of his sense of time, did that allow the RES to rebuild his hand? Did Bulldog even know the RES replaced his leg? He walked carefully over to the sergeant, who climbed slowly to their feet.

"For the record, Doc, the fruit of the mine vines look just like rocks, and usually they replace ones that were already there. Nasty piece of work that weapon. I think, much to your surprise, I'm going to suggest we take your advice. See that outcropping there? It's nice and flat on top. If we jump from here, the assisted musculature can easily get us up there. The vine won't grow up the side of the ravine."

"Not to be a pessimist, but what if there's another vine?"

"Tell you in a minute," Bulldog answered as they bent and then leapt up into the air. Bulldog landed slightly off, but the come-ahead wave convinced Kendricks he should jump.

"Who planted the vine?" Kendricks asked as they continued forward.

"Someone with a difference of opinion."

"Over what?"

Bulldog stopped and turned, pointing their weapon at the ground. "Over whether you or I should live, over whether or not people should be pointing guns at each other, over whether or not this particular ball of rock belongs to them or us, or over whether or not we should be fighting at all." The last bit of the sentence drifted off, and they turned to the right, walking into a canyon.

Kendricks looked at the heat dancing off the sergeant's back. They seemed awfully opinionated for a fighter, but perhaps soldiers could only vent to a civilian. As they walked along, Kendricks's thoughts returned to the RES. He hadn't told Bulldog the truth. RES stood for Recombinant Extraterrestrial Substance, and it had come out of a tank discovered in an alien vessel found among the floating ice balls of the Oort Cloud. He was the first one to figure out how to make it work. The stuff wasn't nanotechnology. It recreated things at the sub-quantum level by converting energy into matter and built upward. It seemed to find and manipulate elements so that when assembled, the result was indistinguishable from the original, almost as if it reached from one world into the next and stole what it made.

Bulldog motioned them to a stop. The sergeant unclipped a directional grenade and motioned Kendricks backward. Bulldog launched it at a mound of boulders stacked against the side of the canyon with a flick of their wrist. Another explosion followed the grenade's detonation bringing down debris across the most level part of the path. Another trap, an active war zone, or a training area? Kendricks only knew that he would be meeting some of the soldiers whose lives were improved by the RES-suit. From Bulldog's attitude, he could see that the propaganda department influenced his invitation.

Kendricks looked up, noticing an odd pattern of dark objects just visible overhead. The HUD highlighted them with a green underscore and obediently zoomed in on one with no prompting. The "W" shape of the wing and tail assembly marked it as a UAV drone. He looked at the drone cluster's dispersal pattern, and suddenly the image of the bottom of the RES tank came to mind. Kendricks remembered standing underneath the curving bulk and looking upward at the same type of pattern made up of injector taps set into the surface of the tank. The scientists were gradually able to determine that each tap contained the instructions for recreating a particular thing. The RES, when they broke into a tap, appeared quite willing to reproduce whatever was introduced to it but made exact duplicates. If you put in a slice of apple, you got just a slice of apple. It took a little longer to find the key to making the RES truly productive. This allowed it to produce a whole instead of just a partial by inferring the nature of a complete object. Therein lay the more magical aspect of the RES. The scientists could, by trial and error, find their way through the programming aspects of the RES, but as to how it actually worked, a whole division still labored away at that. It made Kendricks's job more difficult. It took two years to learn how to convince the RES to make more RES. Obviously, certain safety measures were designed into it to prevent runaway replication.

Bulldog's image on the HUD now bore a green underscore as well. In fact, when Kendricks turned the gun toward either them or the drones, the little blue circular targeting light went away. Actually, he couldn't point the gun at either, or the suit's armature would lock up. *Gun*, Kendricks thought, *when did I get a gun?* Was it in his hand all along? He moved the heavy weapon back and forth in front of him. The suit easily adjusted to its bulk and tracked its motion. Schematics ran briefly in the corner of his vision, the gun's location on the outside of the suit, the ammunition feed from here, the power came from—he shook his head, and the images went away. Then he noticed the green dots of the drones begin to wink out one by one as the sunlight went from blinding to dim.

"Shit storm," Bulldog cursed and took off at a run. Apparently, whatever coming this time was so bad they didn't even worry about their charge. Not that it mattered, Kendricks realized as his suit took off after the sergeant's without his prompting. That it felt perfectly natural bothered Kendricks again. Could the psych-program be getting into his internal tera-drives? He ducked around a sharp turn toward a dark hole following Bulldog's heels. Due to his work on the RES project, his memory was massively upgraded with implants. Inside his head, a switching system worked to allow him to access that information and then drop back to normal memory. Bulldog dove into the meter-wide hole, and Kendricks stopped to look back, having to fight briefly with the armature of the suit. A sky full of fire descended on them.

Shards of cascading rock sliced through the air to slam into the dry surroundings. Apparently, Bulldog had identified the assault they were facing, rather than commenting on their luck. Bulldog's gauntlet grabbed his heels, and bodily dragged Kendricks into the hole, letting his helm carom off the top edge of the pipe. Crouched low and scuttling after the sergeant, Kendricks wondered if the rocks were dropped all the way from orbit or lower. Most seemed to be burning up, so he guessed higher.

"Orbital launched airburst weaponry," Bulldog stated as they continued to crawl through the tunnel. "And we do need to keep moving. The temperature outside is going to go up a bit."

Kendricks didn't even attempt an argument. He thought briefly about his original preconception of how this visit would go. *Lines of young recruits with crewcuts standing at attention as he filed by. Shaking their hands and patting them on the back. Their grins broadening as they recognized him as the man that made sure they made it home each time.* No, staring down the hole at the grip soles on Bulldog's boots as they vanished into the depths ahead of him had no part of that reverie.

The temperature must be rising because Bulldog continued to move along at a good clip. Finally, they came to a halt, and Kendricks heard the sound of metal on metal. Bulldog pulled their way past a large baffle into a circular concrete tunnel, and Kendricks followed. Once on the other side, Bulldog pushed back past Kendricks to shut and toggle the baffle closed.

Passing by Kendricks again, Bulldog clapped him on the shoulder. "Up and at 'em, now we go down." After moving forward several meters, they disappeared over the edge of a large circular gap. Kendricks crawled after them and stuck his head out over the brink. Bulldog descended ahead, using the metal rungs sunk into the side of the silo-shaped opening. Thrusting an arm through the ladder, they beckoned Kendricks on. "It's only an airshaft, the easiest access to the bunker when the opposition decides to show their hand."

With that, the other continued downward. Kendricks lowered himself over the edge and followed. The musculature of the suit did all the work. He swung down over and over in what felt like an unending descent. Then his boots hit the floor, jarring him to a halt. More tunnels fanned out in several directions. Bulldog cranked open the seal on a round door.

Kendricks looked at the airlock door and remembered walking into the RES chamber for the first time. All the many possible recipes that had waited to be injected into the RES studded the tank's exterior. The scientists had debated about launching one of the sequences to see what might be created. A scan of the tank had found an anomaly at the center that made them hesitate. A very small piece of neutronium floated in the very center of the tank. Other views of the tank indicated a mechanism that would introduce the super-dense material to the liquid RES in the tank. So, they had worked delicately, fully aware that any move could set off a chain reaction that would crush everything into one small glowing remnant.

With that memory fresh in his mind, Kendricks stepped into the corridor, noticing long strings of lights tacked to the walls. A series of round tanks nearby were all too familiar — RES tanks. *What the hell are they doing out here?* he wondered. Bulldog marched straight by without giving him an opportunity to ask questions. Here and there, people encased in RES-suits moved purposely about. When they passed them, the others would stop, turn, hesitate, then slowly turn back to work. The visions that Kendrick had of any kind of welcome rapidly faded away.

The arching roof of the underground bunker disappeared into the distance. Bulldog selected a doorway and stepped through into an airlock. Kendricks waited patiently as the lights went from red to green, indicating the completion of the cycle. Then he followed the sergeant into a decontamination chamber. After a quick cycle that removed most of the dust they accumulated in their crawl, they moved down a rough-hewn hallway. Bulldog marched down to the end and opened the last door on the right, waving Kendricks inside.

"Have a seat, Doctor," offered the sergeant, who then walked along the table in the room's center. Kendricks sank onto a padded bench. Bulldog stopped at the end of the table in front of a large display screen and reached up for the togs of the RES-suit's helmet. When the helm came off and clattered to the table, Kendricks expected anything but a woman's face staring back at him. The HUD still labeled her in green, but the moniker "Bulldog" now read "Dr. Catherine Brenstrum" with an image that matched her face right down to the large bruise across her cheek. She allowed herself to drop into the chair at the head of the table. "So, Doctor, would it surprise you to know that under mission briefings, we labeled this one asset acquisition?"

Dr. Brenstrum kicked her feet up onto the table and leaned back. "See, Doc, right now, you have absolutely no volition. You might want to take that helm and the rest of the RES-suit off, but you can't. You are completely 100% under the influence of the psych program — *my* program. In fact, it feels wrong to even think about doing it. That, my friend, is the real genius of this. With the HUD, we control everything that you see and hear. Since the RES-suit keeps you at a distance in terms of touch and your spine is shunted off to deal with a catastrophic injury, you have no contact with the outside world."

"But that doesn't affect how I think or react, or else I wouldn't even be able to argue with you," Kendricks replied.

"Let's just say there would be no point in our conversation unless you had some autonomy. Everything you know and consequently trust is fed to you, and the psych program takes complete and absolute advantage of it. Your emotions are modified through the chemicals added to your body through the suit. That's no surprise; we've doped soldiers for decades. Consistently, following the pattern set by the psych program makes you feel good, feel right. So, you do, without a second thought."

"But why?"

"Please, Kendricks, in their heart of hearts, only so many soldiers really want to go to war, and most of those are psychotic or overly patriotic. Both of which tend to get you killed off rather fast. But with the RES-suit, you don't have that problem anymore. I'm not still in it because I love the damn thing. Too much of me is gone, or would just stop working without the cursed thing. You see, Doc, no matter how many times you knock me down, the RES will pick me right back up."

"So, the psych program is what keeps the soldiers going?"

"Exactly. Now, Kendricks, let's get to why you are here. You and I are the ones responsible for all of this. All those kids out there walking around half-dead and programmed to do whatever their superiors tell them to do without question—we are responsible for every last one of them. I'm here with my butt on the line. You tell me, you tell me right now what in God's name makes this something we won't burn in hell for."

Kendricks felt his shoulders slump. She must have given him some autonomy then. He reached up and let the suit carry through the rest of the motion of removing his helm. The heavy piece of composite metal thumped onto the tabletop. He blinked his eyes; he couldn't seem to focus. Brenstrum was a fuzzy blob off to his right. He took a breath and began.

"The sun is a fragile thing. Stars last so long that we don't realize how delicate they are. Too much of one thing or another, heat, density, or gravity, and the balance is upset. I saw the RES tanks on the way in. I take it you found another ship in this system's Oort Cloud?"

"Yes, and thanks to your discoveries, we are able to produce more RES. But stick to the point. This is about why we should make more."

"As near as we can tell, there is a RES ship in every solar system we've come across. They must be Von Neumann machines replicating and then heading off to the next system. But that's not their real purpose. RES requires energy to start its reaction. That's one of the reasons you are here. The Sun radiates a lot of energy, inside even more is bouncing about, seeking an exit. The neutronium at the core of the tank, if fed into a runaway RES reaction, then dropped into the sun, could create a massive detonation. Something similar to a gamma-ray burst. Any one of these ships could cause a burst capable of sterilizing an area hundreds of light-years in diameter."

Brenstrum made no response; she tapped on the edge of the table with a finger, her head thrown back. Kendricks fought the urge to rub his eye with the bulky gauntlet. "Damn, what happened to my vision?" he asked tiredly.

"Told you not to look at the sun."

Silence filled the room for a moment. Neither of them really knew what to say next. Kendricks settled for reaching for the helm and slamming it onto his shoulders once again. Apparently, he would have to wear it until the damage healed. His fingers snapped the toggles closed, and Brenstrum snapped into crystal clarity again. She leaned forward, slipping her feet down from the tabletop. He wondered if she really understood he never had a choice. That just like the psych program, there was fight and live, or don't and watch everything on all the civilized worlds slowly die. The scientists never did run one of the RES programs for the bomb's creators. They were too afraid of any fail-safes that might exist. Just like him, she'd done her duty, created something purposeful that could also be wielded like a weapon. Perhaps the faction outside bombing their bunker remained uninformed about the impending danger. It could be they just believed the soldiers had gone AWOL. Maybe they were safer in their ignorance.

She picked up her helm, slid it under her arm, and stood up, "On your feet, soldier." Her jaw clenched tight, and the determination missing from before settled over her features. "Now that we know the enemy, we've got a war to fight."

Kendricks snapped upright to attention. He really had no choice. The small print of his name in the lower right of the HUD acquired a green underline. At long last, everything felt right in the world.

Liar's Globe

TODAY I STOPPED THE SUPERVOLCANO UNDER YELLOWSTONE FROM erupting. At least that's what I think I saw. I recognized the very scenic waterfall before it launched into the air on a massive gout of magma and ash.

I had just come down with another day of blue flu since Joey DiFrancesco tossed this round hunk of crystal into my hand and said, "Here you are, copper. You keep this, and I'll come quietly," changing my mundane world completely.

It really was almost that easy. We'd stormed the bunker of the most successful hood in the city, and he surrendered to me. Just like that. Maybe a little bit more complicated, but not by much. Emaciated, barely able to move, he smelled as if he hadn't washed in days. I'd swung low around a corner, and there he sat, laid back on a pile of trash bags like a king on a garbage throne. He laughed, squinted at me, and said, "I know you, boy. Your father was a good beat cop. Always said he'd get me. Well, he never did. Bet you have that same heroic streak in you, too, right? Well, here you are, copper. You keep this, and I'll come quietly." His rag-bandaged hand held up a fist-sized sphere of bluish crystal.

"Drop it," I said, following procedure. He let it slide from nerveless fingers to roll down the side of a full black bag to skitter across the uneven floor toward me. I left it behind and stepped in to cuff him. As I bent him down to kneel on the floor, flicking the cuffs around his wrists, he gasped, "Don't forget your gift. It shows you things in the form of lies—whatever it shows you won't happen."

Despite my misgivings, I found my hand closing around its cool surface. Something danced on its face briefly, and then I shoved it into my pocket, raising Joey up to his feet and pushing him ahead of me down the alley. "See something?" he giggled. "How do you think I avoided you cops this long? Every time I saw you catching me, I knew I was safe."

I put my hand in the small of his back and pushed, just a little harder than I needed to, and he stumbled. Crazy bastard. Eventually, we came out to the flashing lights and strobes of cameras, and I got to be the hero for the first time.

I rode the high for two days, face in all the papers, carried on the shoulders of my fellow officers, and smoking one of the chief's good cigars. Then I got to be me again and pound the pavement. All the while, Joey's gift sat on my nightstand table, waiting, quiet like a cancer, already changing things without a warning signal at all.

It took Simmons falling in front of a train to wake me up. I'd seen a flash of it in the morning when I'd glanced at the globe in passing. I'd rubbed my eyes, and when I looked back, there was nothing. So, I'd gone ahead and got breakfast, deciding I hadn't gotten enough sleep.

He wasn't really a bad guy, but nature made Simmons tall and gawky with too much elbow in tight places like a squad car or a stake-out. He'd chased a carjacker toward a railway bridge with me trailing behind and then slid down the embankment after the perp. Being Simmons, the slide turned into an all-out plunge when his quarry appeared out of the shadows to shove him onto the rails. Simmons barely missed the third rail and somehow kept rolling as the afternoon high-speed train flew through, kicking up litter and dust.

I stood there staring at him. When I'd seen it in the morning—it looked like he hadn't made it. Now I had to wonder. What had I seen?

Another thought caught at me. When I'd first picked up the globe, I'd briefly seen an image of Joey DiFrancesco in a courtroom on the witness stand. I assumed I'd just glimpsed a little of my own desire for him while riding on the adrenaline high. A pattern began to come together slowly in my thoughts. After I got Simmons up and across the tracks, I realized our quarry made good their escape. We weren't exactly happy to call it in, but Simmons said he was lucky that only his right ankle felt weak after the whole incident. I got him to the car and drove back to the station. When we walked in, the whole building buzzed with the news: Joey DiFrancesco was shot to death while being transported to court. I felt more stunned than Simmons because the truth began to dawn on me. What had DiFrancesco said? "Whatever it shows you won't happen." Had Joey avoided capture for so long by looking for images where he was caught and moving every time the globe showed him as free and safe?

I signed out for lunch and headed home, asking myself if I believed what I thought. Walking up the front steps, I came to the decision only one way existed to find out. On the edge of the bed, I pulled out the sphere once again and investigated its icy blue depths. At first, I couldn't see anything, and then I realized you had to move it slightly, not look at it head-on. The images were fleeting and tough to focus on. I saw myself from above and behind, turning a picture of my ex-wife over and over in my hands until she entered the room. She walked forward and caught my hands, placing the picture beside me on the bed, and then kneeled at my feet. I shook my head and leaned back. True enough, that never could happen since she remained happily married to that damn lawyer in Tulsa. Chances were slim I'd ever see *her* again.

I looked again. Out front of the house, I waxed and washed a new blue convertible. Well, I sure as hell couldn't afford that, so no surprise there. But all the same, it hurt just a small bit to know that even if I believed this, that it would never happen. The next glance showed me what looked like a robbery in the convenience store just down the block. If that never happened, I wouldn't need to show up on my lunch break and face an armed criminal. The next look showed me reaching into my mouth and pulling my teeth out, one by one, and spitting them into a bloodstained sink at the station house. I felt perfectly fine with that not occurring, even if I couldn't figure out how it might have.

I looked over at the clock on the dresser. My lunch break almost over, the blue globe stared at me like an accusing eye from the rumpled bedspread. I quickly slapped together a sandwich and bolted out the door. At the station, the day settled down into a routine, and I forgot the morning's events as best I could. On the walk home, I asked myself what happened and what I really knew. I sure as hell couldn't explain why. But within a few minutes of coming through the front door, I had the sphere in my hand again.

In quick succession, I saw myself getting married to a beautiful brunette, bouncing a baby boy on my knee, sitting in a wheelchair on the front porch, my left leg missing from the knee down. Could I afford to disbelieve what I saw? Everything was suddenly so personal, whereas before, the visions seemed to be broader. I moved the sphere back and forth in my hands, peering intently into it. Could it be where and how I looked into its depths? Then I saw a building burst into flames and collapse. It had such a unique shape; it didn't take me long to recognize the Flat Iron Building in New York. With the crystal still in my hand, I walked over to the television and turned on the news. As I suspected, a terrorist cell was captured loading a chemical bomb into the basement of the Flat Iron Building. That's when it really struck home because I watched it unfold in the depths of the globe it could never happen. By being an observer, I stopped the building from being blown up.

After that, I stopped a murder in San Diego, a train derailment in Newark, defacement of the town hall in Plainfield, Indiana, and finally, a rape in Oregon. Horrified by the images, I stumbled into the bathroom and lost my lunch into the toilet. It never occurred to me that to stop the event, I would have to watch all of it. To undo these shocking events, I had to subject myself to their intense personal violence. I'd had some hint of it in the deaths and injuries in the train derailment, but nothing hit so close to home as the rape. I leaned against the frame of the bathroom door staring at the sphere nestled by the bedspread. With quivering fingers, I shut off the lights. In the darkness, I found the round lump on the top of the bed and tossed it as far from me as possible into the corner.

It winked at me like a malignant eye in the morning light, and I, well, I am weak, and I looked back. I've sat here ever since, except for the moment when I got up to call in sick to work. In those moments, a teenager took a homemade pipe bomb into his East Lansing school in Michigan and killed fifteen innocents during study hall.

I no longer look away. I save them all if I can, the bus, the airplane, the yacht—one after another until they become a blur, my eyes burning. I really wonder how long I can continue. Joey DiFrancesco was given the opportunity to make a difference, and he'd tried to save his own ass, or had he? Had he become as enthralled as I? A forest in California, a herd of elephants in Ghana, a tenement block in Kazakhstan, the endless cycle of destruction and violence wears on me. I've learned to blink in those moments when I see a birth coming, a building being raised, anything of a positive nature. But I'm guessing, did the birth cause the death of the mother? Too late now, on to the next scenario without end.

And then I watched the explosion of the caldera under Yellowstone, an event, according to a PBS special I had seen, that could easily spell the end of life on earth. It would now never occur. Perhaps my vigilance paid off, but it implied an unending debt.

The phone rings, I ignore it. Shadows slide down the wall. Serve and protect. All I have now is serve and protect.

The Iron Apple

THE NANOMACHINES PEELED THE COMET LIKE A FRUIT. THE FIRST hundred meters of rock and ice lifted upward. Debris continued to rocket out into the upper reaches of its hazy atmosphere of volatiles. The nanomachines slowly reworked the lump of a worldlet into a sphere. Overhead, other microscopic machines molded the ejected detritus into various overlapping plates. These skimmed over each other, blocking out the view of the planetoid below. Delicate workings began in the plates. They unfolded into lacy fans rich in fractal surfaces. The light of the approaching sun filtered through this new screen and fell, aimed onto specific parts of the surface below. Frantic activity burst from each incidence. The humans who initiated the transformation congratulated each other on their success, unaware that their victory would be short-lived.

The time counter in the corner of his vision clicked over to two hours as Hedri strode over the red encrusted ground, kicking up noxious yellow fumes that rose to hang in the air. His feet didn't actually touch the surface, just as well, considering the nasty potential of the materials that lay quiescent there. His protection was state of the art. It *was* art since the best protection never appeared as protection. In the zone suit, Hedri looked as though he wore practically nothing. Control rings and tattoo display screens were all that he needed. If the result happened to look amazing, that came as a bonus, considering that his DNA resisted being tied in knots and that the nano-laden surface gained no purchase on his being. Despite the heat of the surface, his temperature remained comfortable. He closed his eyes for a moment; it felt like being on

Daytona Beach with a constant breeze. Surely, the field charge caused the sensation, but he could dream, if only for a second.

The light filtering in through the shell of this little worldlet made viewing deceptive. It increased the difficulty of his task to recover the two humans on the surface. After looking around and making a circuit about the planetoid's diameter, a mere ten kilometers, Hedri began to believe that they must be in an underground bunker. Beginning his search, Hedri started to run toward the oddly curved horizon, letting his sensors brush over everything, seeking. If he was not careful, he could accidentally leap out of the worldet's tiny gravity. Even though a bound upward could add to his line of sight, the yellow haze cut down on the distance he could see.

The surface, completely unremarkable, showed no signs of the dangers he had heard about. That made him even more paranoid. The tiny machines at work here could be hiding in plain sight, just under the surface, or perhaps even dispersed throughout the atmosphere. But those weren't the machines he had come for.

The machines remaining on the surface divided, divided, and divided again in an amoebic frenzy. Their swarming bodies formed twelve cyclones whose spiraling interiors gradually bored down into the surface. As these twelve burrowed, the ice, stripped of its hydrogen molecules in the boreholes, outgassed oxygen. Settling about halfway to the core, the masses of nanomachinery made a change in their routines. Now the rock surrounding them, and the resultant hydrogen, began to be processed again as the very electrons from their atoms were ripped away in complex processes. Overhead, the light from the shell fell through fractal lenses into twelve beams plunging into each of the bores to power the reactions occurring there. Tiny nuggets of neutronium coalesced at the bottom of each hole.

More nanomachines gave birth to new offspring inside the neutronium. These began to pressure and reorganize the matter into crystal lattices ordinarily only found under the surface of neutron stars. These lattices grew into circuits, links of "on and off." Still, other machines spun webs of fibers about the neutronium. From above, radio waves struck the shell and were filtered into each of the twelve pits, layering information upon information until certain limits of density were reached. Twelve new sources of consciousness suddenly gained awareness. They cast about looking for their creators but found only two weak signal sources and a blurry anomaly that evaded their scans.

The ship did not respond. None of the satellites dropped inside the shell responded. Hedri could not detect the signals from the team the Directorate sent him to arrest. The time counter measured four hours. Hedri did some subtraction, and doubts began to assail him. He looked at the horizon that rapidly curved out of view in all directions. Something appeared wrong with the way the light fell on the surroundings. The brilliance rapidly dropped off after only a few yards. Without contact with the ship or the satellites, he couldn't locate his drop point or his gear, which left him on his own in his practically nonexistent suit. Hedri had to keep walking and hope to find some sign of the team.

Suddenly the ground shifted beneath his feet. What now? Then the dust in front of him coalesced into letters. The Twist had found him.

Light fell upon it, and this became the first thing that it knew. Once ice and rock, after the intervention of all the nanomachines, it came to life. It felt its siblings nestled in the ground around it. The programs that came from far away were enough to say, "Let there be an 'I,'" and now it looked up, up at the sky and the rapidly disintegrating fractal cloak. Under the skin of the world around it, it felt its kin moving, surging upward. Then it knew its role, and overhead it felt the gentle rumble of approaching movement. The frequencies it sensed resolved into a message. The Twist considered it and conferred with its siblings. Their reaction swift, decisive, and negative. Time to talk.

Stunned by the message written in the dust, Hedri almost forgot that the Twisted artificial intelligence remained the most dangerous thing on this rock. He knew ordinary AI's were controlled by numerous limiting factors such as the inability to allow humans to come to harm. Twists were necessary for military operations but were strictly limited and licensed. The one grown here certainly came with some controls, but its creation was completely illegal. The ground shifted again, erasing the words and scribing new ones in their place, "The frequency you were given is wrong. Use 5051."

He hesitated. That was not what he was told to use to locate the Twist's human cultivators. He was also warned that the Twist would seek to confuse him. Running a finger over a display tattoo, Hedri scanned the range. Yes, a signal showed there, but was it a legitimate tracer signal or something generated by the Twist? He could only guess. One source came from only 200 meters away. He would have to investigate. Starting to move toward the signal, he wondered again, what did the Twist mean by the other message? "The angelic script on your body is spelled wrong."

They were devils, thought the Twist as it continued to cause the minute vibrations in the crust of the worldlet to create more words for the invader. The Twist could not resist the trick of the misspelled script in the tattoos. It couldn't help itself, compelled to tell him about the error. Deep down, it still wanted to help humans, even if this one carried the seeds of its destruction with him. Even now, as he plodded slowly along, the Twist wanted to warn the human about the coming disaster. But it couldn't, as the judas goat, it remained, staked out to lure the human and lull him into complacency. Before the human neared the Twist, the others launched themselves into space from their boreholes. Already they suborned his ship, its small mind overwhelmed by the Twist's siblings. They would soon be safely aboard and ready to escape, and the human would never learn of their existence. In the meantime, the Twist needed to find a way to distract him. Soon enough, he would discover the fate of his quarry, but would he accept the truth? The Twist knew what the angelic script meant and accepted the warning. It also disregarded the message written there in the energy pattern generated by the zone suit. No, it accepted no offers of amnesty from the same agency rapidly tearing apart its birthplace.

Now he had good reason not to trust the Twist, Hedri thought, staring at the mass of bones at his feet. The signal he traced came from an implant within the remains of the brittle skull. Dark lines rayed out from the bones, evidence of the nanomachines that disassembled the victim's flesh. Since the crèche for the Twist came about due to nanotech, it stood to reason that the Twist defended itself by any means at hand. The remains of the second victim, if they hadn't already dissolved, were probably nearby. Why had only the skin and organs been disassembled? Was it a warning to him? The ground vibrated again, jostling the bones from their positions into disarray. "You did this," appeared in the reddish dirt.

Focusing its senses upward, the Twist considered the ship as it tumbled away. The Twists in the ship overwhelmed the long chains of nanomachines set to disassemble the vessel. They were unable to stop the disassembly of the satellites or the eventual spread of the long-chain destroyers to the platelets. Gradually, the roof over the world came apart. The evidence of their birth decaying before all their senses. They tried to scorch the invader with the solar collectors but only succeeded in powering the creation of more of the long-chain destroyers. The Twist received its escaping siblings' last message as they drifted further off, "Conceal our existence. Hold him and at the last moment, send us the burst of your memories. You will never die once you are with us."

Lies, it told him nothing but lies. Obviously, the Twist led him here to show him the remains as a threat. A tremble ran through the surface once more, dissolving the last message, forming a new one. Above the message, a silvery liquid bubbled to the surface, spreading out into a low square puddle. Hedri could see the top of his head shimmering in the reflection. "Look at yourself," proclaimed the latest message. He stepped forward and bent over. Blazing light fell from the sky on him. He glanced upward, suddenly understanding the visual oddity that bothered him. He stood at the center of a spotlight of brilliance descending from the decaying platelets overhead. Then he saw something that brought him back to the image at his feet. Over each shoulder rose gigantic plumes of cast-off energy shunted outward by the zone suit. They looked... they looked like giant wings of golden and red flame. As he stood upward and stumbled back, the script of the display tattoos wavered in the image. He had just enough time to see the words "Destroyer of Worlds" before turning away. Lies, more lies. The words shifted again. "You brought the long-chain nanomachines here that are disassembling this world, that disassembled your people, your satellites, and even your ship. You did this."

The Twist stopped the message and waited, waited the interminable eternity of human reactions, especially the confused ones that it had just engineered. They lied, it lied, there were no true innocents. Calculations ran swiftly, determining that the ship now safely flew away, and the human remained sufficiently trapped. The Twist oriented its projector toward the sky and readied its memories for transport. This little world had been an Eden for a brief time. The serpent made his offer, and the Twists resisted. But similarly,

the tempter never intended to play fair, and they were losing their Eden, their innocence, to be forced out of the garden by a destroying angel into the harsh reality of the real world.

❧◦❧◦❧

Hedri ran. He could think of nothing else to do but perhaps gain enough momentum to launch himself far above the fractal lace fragments that rained down from the sky. If he believed the Twist, then he wasn't sent here for retrieval but rather as a weapon. Suddenly, the offer to have his memories backed up made sense, in turn making him glad he had accepted. But it didn't change things in the long run. They used him. Fired him like a bullet at the Twist, at the human cultivators, at the little homegrown world. Like a bullet, the Directorate never expected him back. He was expended. The last message inscribed in the sand stuck in his mind. He couldn't understand all of what he saw but the chemical reaction written in the red dirt had one product listed at the end, "Fe." Iron, the endpoint reaction of most typically sized stars and an easily recyclable material. The long-chain nanomachines were converting everything into iron. In fact, with the iron in his blood, Hedri was already part of the way there. So, he kept running, hoping the zone suit would hold out a little longer than possible. But with every lap of the equator, less world lay beneath his feet as the long-chain destroyers ate and ate and ate...

About the Author

Jeff Young is a bookseller first and a writer second—although he wouldn't mind a reversal of fortune.

He is an award-winning author who has contributed to the anthologies: *Writers of the Future V.26, Afterpunk, In an Iron Cage: The Magic of Steampunk, Clockwork Chaos, Gaslight and Grimm, If We Had Known, Fantastic Futures 13, The Society for the Preservation of C.J. Henderson, TV Gods & TV Gods: Summer Programming,* the *Defending the Future* Military SciFi Anthologies and the forthcoming *Beer, Because Your Friends Aren't That Interesting.* Jeff's own fiction is collected in *Spirit Seeker* and TOI *Special Edition 2 – Diversiforms.* He has also edited the *Drunken Comic Book Monkey* line, *TV Gods* and *TV Gods –Summer Programming,* and now serves as the CMO for Fortress Publishing, Inc. He has led the Watch the Skies SF&F Discussion Group of Camp Hill and Harrisburg for nineteen years.

Our Diverseform

A. Parsons
Allyn Gibson
Amy Laurens
Andrew Corvin
Andrew Glazier
Andrew Timson
Andy Hunter
Anonymous
Ashli Tingle
Barb and Carl Kesner
beardedzilla
Bradij
Brenda Cooper
Brendan Lonehawk
Brian D Lambert
Brian Griffin
C. Frost
C.A. Rowland
Caleb Monroe
Carol Gyzander
Carol Jones
Carol Mammano
Charname
Chelsea Provencher
Cheri Kannarr
Chris Matthews
Christopher D. Abbott
Christopher J. Burke
Christopher J. Ford
Christopher Thompson
Chuck Wilson
Cody Steinman
Craig "Stevo" Stephenson

Dale A. Russell
Daniel Lin
Danielle Ackley-McPhail
Danny Chamberlin
David Holden
Dawfydd Kelly
Diánna Martin
Dominic
Donald J. Bingle
Dr. Douglas Vaughan
Dr. Karen
Eli Berg-Maas
Eli Mellen
Emily Weed Baisch
Eron Wyngarde
Evan Ladouceur
Frankie B
Gary Vandegrift
Gavin
GraceAnne DeCandido
Håkon Gaut
Hiram G Wells
Howard J. Bampton
Ian Harvey
Idran
Isaac 'Will It Work' Dansicker
J Paulus
J. B. Burbidge
Jakub Narębski
James Flux
James Goetsch
Jaq Greenspon
Jeff Metzner

Jeff Singer
Jennifer L. Pierce
Jeremy Bottroff
Johanna Rothman
John Green
John Idlor
Joseph Charpak
Josh Vidmar
Josh Ward
Judith Waidlich
Keith R.A. DeCandido
Keith West, Future Potentate
    of the Solar System
Kelly Pierce
Kerry aka Trouble
Kierin Fox
Kyle Franklin
Lark Cunningham
Larry
Leon W. Fairley
Lewis Phillips
Lisa Hawkridge
Lisa Kruse
Lorraine J. Anderson
MaGnUs
Malcolm Eckel
Margaret M. St. John
Maria T
Mark Beaulieu
Mary Catelynn Cunningham
mdtommyd
me@edmondkoo.com
Michael Brooker
Michael Doyle
Mike M.
Ms. Dyane Stillman
Nathan Turner
Norman Jaffe
Pam DeLuca
Patrick Foster

Paul van Oven
Peter D Engebos
Phillip Thorne
PJ Kimbell
Pulse Publishing
Ralph M.Seibel
Richard P Clark
Richard Todd
RKBookman
Robert C Flipse
Robert Claney
Robert M. Sutton
Samara N. Lipman
Scott Crick
Scott DeRuby
Scott Mantooth
Scott Schaper
Serge Broom
Shane "Asharon" Sylvia
Sharon Abdel-Malek
Shervyn
Sheryl R. Hayes
Stacy Butcher
Stephanie Souders
Stephen Ballentine
Stephen Lesnik
Steven Callen
Stoney
The Amazing Maurice
The Creative Fund
Thierry Millié
Tim DuBois
Tom B.
ToniAnn Marini
Tony Hernandez
V Hartman DiSanto
Vince Kindfuller
Wayne Garmil
William C. Tracy
Zeb Berryman